THE FAIRY TALES OF
Hans Christian Andersen

First published by Parragon Books Ltd in 2015

Parragon Books Ltd
Chartist House
15–17 Trim Street
Bath BA1 1HA, UK
www.parragon.com

Illustrated by Victoria Assanelli, Livia Coloji, Charlotte Cooke,
Dawn Cooper, Ciaran Duffy, Katy Hudson, Ayesha Lopez,
Polona Lovsin, Ada Pianura, Karissa Santos, Kristina Swarner,
Jenny Wren and Aleksander Zolotic.

Edited by Mandy Archer and Michael Diggle
Designed by Duck Egg Blue and Karissa Santos
Production by Emma Fulleylove

ISBN 978-1-4723-9176-6

Printed in China

THE FAIRY TALES OF

Hans Christian Andersen

RETOLD BY
MANDY ARCHER

PaRragon

Bath · New York · Cologne · Melbourne · Delhi
Hong Kong · Shenzhen · Singapore · Amsterdam

Contents

The Little Mermaid

Far, far out to sea, where the water is crystal clear, lies a secret kingdom. Here, countless leagues below the waves, a thousand mer-people swim, chatter and play. It is a dazzling realm of dancing light, glittering shoals of fish and coral reefs that bloom in emerald, crimson and gold.

The mer-king's palace was in the very deepest part of the ocean. Its majestic walls were topped with shells that opened and closed with the tides. The tall, domed windows were made from glinting amber. On calm days the windows were thrown open, allowing little fish to dart inside, just as birds might above the surface. Outside the palace there was a magnificent garden, filled with rows of swaying sea-trees.

Although the mer-king's wife had died many years ago, he had six sweet daughters. The mer-king loved to watch them swimming in the palace garden, tending the plants and petting the little fish that swam up to greet them. Each of the six princesses was fair, but the youngest was the most beautiful of all. Her eyes sparkled blue like the ocean. Instead of feet, her body tapered into a shimmering tail.

The youngest princess was a quiet, wistful girl with a gentle heart. While her sisters chattered with their friends she would swim amongst the sea-flowers, dreaming of faraway adventures. Sometimes she would seek out her beloved grandmother, who would tell her stories about the other world far above them – the place where the waves meet the shore.

"What is it like on the land?" the little mermaid used to ask.

The old mer-queen would think for a moment.

"The human world is strange and spectacular," she would answer. "It is full of cities and towns, beaches and fields. Up there, even the flowers are different. On the land they have a sweet perfume, yet down here they have none."

As her grandmother talked, the little mermaid would try to imagine what it must be like to walk on two legs and feel the breeze on her face. She longed to dance like a human girl, to see the sun twinkling through the clouds and to hear birds singing in the trees.

"Once a mermaid is fifteen," said her grandmother, "she is allowed to swim up to the surface. Be patient, little one. Your turn will come. One day you will sit on the rocks and stare out across the waves. You'll see great ships sail by and watch the seagulls hover overhead. You might even see the land curving around the shore."

The little mermaid flipped her tail at such an exciting thought! A flurry of sparkling bubbles danced and bobbed around her. Soon it would be the little mermaid's eldest sister's fifteenth birthday – her chance to swim up to the surface for the first time. Each of the princesses was a year older than the next. It would be another five years before the little mermaid could discover what the human world was like.

When the eldest princess's birthday arrived, the little mermaid made her sister promise to come back and tell her everything that she saw.

"I swam up and up," the eldest princess told her sisters when she returned. "When I pushed my head out through the waves, the sky

was bright with sunshine. The air felt warm against my cheek. It was so beautiful!"

"What about the land?" asked the little mermaid. "Did you see the land?"

The eldest princess nodded. She described the glint of the harbour and the sounds of a village standing by the shore.

"I heard people shouting in the streets, carriage wheels turning over the cobbles and church bells ringing. Oh, the church bells! I shall never forget their chimes."

The little mermaid listened to every word. The human world sounded more wonderful than ever. That night in her palace chamber, she sat by the window and gazed up through the indigo waters. If she closed her eyes tight, she could almost hear the echo of those church bells chiming far above her. How she longed one day to hear them for herself!

Every year one of the little mermaid's sisters took their turn to swim up to the surface. The second princess told of golden sunsets and purple-tinted clouds. The third princess was more daring. She swam into a tiny cove and saw human children paddling on the beach. She described how they ran up to the waves, giggling every time the foam tickled their toes.

The fourth princess stayed far out to sea. She told the little mermaid about the huge ships that swept past her. The princess watched the vessels pitch through the waves while sailors clung to the rigging.

The fifth princess's birthday was in the winter. The little mermaid trembled as her sister told of massive icebergs that loomed out of the water. Each one was as tall as a cathedral and glittered like diamonds.

Now the little mermaid was the only sea princess who could not visit the human world. When her five sisters held hands and floated up to the surface to sit side by side on the rocks and sing to the ships that sailed by, she was left all alone down below. The poor little mermaid swam round and round the palace gardens, yearning to be with them.

"If only my birthday would come now," she said wistfully. "I am going to love the world up above, I just know it!"

At last the little mermaid was fifteen. Her grandmother brushed her dark brown hair, then plaited it with scallop shells and creamy pearls.

"Now you are ready," she said kindly. "You have come of age."

All of the other sea princesses gathered around their little sister. The little mermaid waved to them as she floated up towards the surface. She felt as light and sparkling as a bubble of air rising through the water.

"Goodbye," she called in her beautiful singsong voice. "See you soon!"

When the little mermaid finally pushed her face out through the salty swell, it was evening. The sun was setting on the horizon. The little mermaid saw the sky for the first time ever, lit up in lilac, pink and gold. Her eyes sparkled with happiness.

"Oh!" she gasped suddenly. "A ship!"

A fine galleon drifted across the horizon. Somewhere inside a band was playing a jaunty tune. Sailors were singing on the deck.

The little mermaid swam closer. As the waves lapped against the sides of the ship, she peeped in through one of the glass windows. Inside she could see men and women dancing together. They were dressed in fine satin ballgowns, lace ruffles and magnificent plumed hats. A young prince with a golden crown walked amongst them, bowing to the ladies and gentlemen that he passed. When he turned towards the window, the little mermaid's heart leapt. The prince was handsome and elegant, with coal-black eyes that glittered in the lamplight.

The band struck up another tune and everyone formed a circle around the prince, clapping and singing.

"It must be his birthday, just like me!" laughed the little mermaid.

Fizz! Sparkle! Zing!

Suddenly a rocket streaked across the sky. The little mermaid dived under the water, and when she mustered the courage to put her head above the waves again, she couldn't believe her eyes. The sky was lit up as bright as day. Cascades of gold and scarlet fireworks showered above her.

The prince and his friends had come onto the deck to enjoy the display.

"If only I could hear what they are saying," she whispered. "I'll swim a little closer."

The little mermaid flicked her tail, but the swell was bigger now. Every time she tried to swim towards the ship, the waves kept her away. A menacing rumble came from deep down below the surface of the ocean.

A storm was on its way.

The fireworks stopped. The ship pitched and rolled. Dark, brooding clouds gathered overhead and lightning split the sky. Timbers creaked as the sailors battled against the wind and rain. Suddenly the ocean lifted the ship high like a child's toy, before sending it lurching down towards the inky waters. There was a terrible crack as the main mast snapped in two.

The little mermaid watched in horror as torn sails and broken beams showered down into the water around her. The ship was starting to sink.

"Where is the prince?" she cried breathlessly, scanning the debris. "I must save him!"

She dived in and out of the waves, over and over again. At the last moment she spotted him. His eyes were closed. The little mermaid cradled the prince in her arms, taking care to keep his face above the waves.

It was a long, perilous night. When the storm finally calmed, the little mermaid found that she and the prince were being washed towards a deserted beach. The sun rose in the sky.

She laid the prince out on the sand, shaping a little pillow for his head. Slowly, the sunlight started to revive him.

"Please live," whispered the sea princess, kissing him gently.

A church bell rang. The little mermaid leapt back into the surf. A girl ran down onto the beach, crying out in surprise when she noticed the fine young man lying by the water's edge. She called for others to help as the prince slowly opened his eyes.

"Where am I?" he asked, blinking at the girl.

From a distance, the little mermaid watched the prince smiling at the people on the beach. She felt sad to think that there was no smile for her. How would he ever know that she was the one who had saved him?

From that moment on, something changed in the little mermaid. Her grandmother watched her sitting in the palace garden, her eyes filled with sadness. The little mermaid could think of nothing except the handsome prince with the coal-black eyes. Sometimes she swam up to the surface, hoping to glimpse him walking along the water's edge. Her heart ached to see him again.

The other sea princesses didn't like to see their little sister looking so forlorn.

"This prince," wondered the eldest princess, "did he have dark eyes, a fine figure and shiny black hair?"

The little mermaid nodded eagerly. "Do you know who he is?"

"Come with us," said the eldest princess. The little mermaid's sisters took her arms and they rose up together through the swirling waters.

"Look over there," said the eldest princess, pointing to a marble palace. "That is the palace where your prince lives."

The little mermaid swam out to a smooth rock below the palace balcony. She sat and waited. It was many hours before someone appeared. Suddenly the little mermaid's heart jumped with joy – there was her prince, leaning over the balcony! He was every bit as handsome as she remembered.

After that, the little mermaid visited the palace every day. She liked it best when the prince stood alone on his balcony looking out to sea.

"How I wish that I were human," she sighed. "I would give anything to be standing up there. I would love to dance and walk beside my handsome prince!"

As time went on, the ache in the little mermaid's heart grew stronger and stronger. The mer-king and his daughters did everything they could to make her smile again. They held balls and banquets, parties and feasts in her honour, but nothing worked.

One day, the little mermaid could not bear it any longer. She secretly stole out of the royal palace, then darted towards the murky depths at the very edge of her father's kingdom.

"I shall visit the sea witch," she said to herself. "Perhaps she can help me."

Everyone knew of the mighty and terrible sea witch, but few had actually seen her. To get to her cold and dingy lair the little mermaid had to swim through raging whirlpools, eerie chasms and dark forests filled with snapping eels. This was the ocean's graveyard. As she passed, the little mermaid shivered at the sight of wrecked ships, forgotten chests and the skeletons of sailors lost long ago.

The little mermaid came to a cave guarded by two enormous water snakes. The serpents writhed on their foul bellies, flicking their tongues at her. This was the sea witch's lair. When a screech rang out from inside the cave, the water snakes moved away from the entrance.

"Hello?" called the little mermaid, swimming inside. "May I enter?"

The sea witch peered out of the gloom. She had been expecting the little mermaid.

"I already know what you want," she said, pointing to a rock jutting out beside a bubbling black cauldron. The little mermaid sat down.

"You wish to shed your sparkling tail and walk like a human girl," continued the sea witch. "Is that right?"

The little mermaid nodded earnestly.

The sea witch threw back her head and cackled. "You foolish creature!" she spat. "But who am I to disappoint a princess? You want to win the prince's love. In fact, you dream of nothing else! I can help you... for a price."

"What can I give you?" began the little mermaid, looking confused.

The sea witch's eyes narrowed. She wanted the most precious thing that the little mermaid possessed – her voice. The witch had heard how sweetly the mer-king's youngest daughter could sing. She would take nothing less.

"I will give you a potion to change your mermaid's tail into the human legs you so desire. But when you walk on the land," warned the sea witch, "every step will cut like the blade of a knife."

The little mermaid's face turned pale. But as her heart thumped in her chest, she solemnly nodded her head.

"You will look as lovely as any human girl," continued the sea witch. "But if you fail to win the prince's love everything will be lost. The first

morning after he marries another, you will melt into sea foam and be gone forever."

The sea witch took a flask from her shelf, then plunged it into the bubbling cauldron. The glass filled with a fiery, rust-coloured liquid. The little mermaid darted out of the sea witch's cave, clutching the flask in her trembling hand.

The little mermaid swam back towards her home. Only the fishes came out to greet her – everyone else was still fast asleep.

"Goodbye, dear father," murmured the little mermaid. "Goodbye grandmother, goodbye sweet sisters. I love you so very much!"

With that, the little mermaid flicked her shimmering tail and set off for the surface. When she reached the shore, she uncorked the sea witch's flask. The potion tasted bitter and foul, but she drank down every drop.

Crash!

A bolt of pain sent the little mermaid tumbling. Her body felt as if it were splitting in two! She fainted onto the sand. When she opened her eyes again, someone was there beside her.

"Please let me help you," said a gentle voice.

The little mermaid gasped. The prince was putting his arms around her and lifting her off the ground! Where there had once been a mermaid's tail, she now had an elegant pair of human legs.

The prince introduced himself politely. The little mermaid desperately tried to reply, but it was hopeless – she could not utter a single word. The sea witch's promise had come true.

All she could do was nod, her eyes burning with anguish. The little mermaid's voice was lost forever.

The gallant young man led her up to his marble palace, intrigued by the beautiful stranger. As soon as the little mermaid arrived, the ladies of the court found a silk gown for her to change into. She looked like a vision, even though she could not speak or sing. Soon everyone in the palace was talking about the mysterious, silent stranger.

The royal court seemed foreign and strange, but the little mermaid did not miss her watery home. She even got used to walking on two legs. Every step cut like a blade, but it was worth the pain. Wherever the prince went, he took the little mermaid with him. They rode and walked, travelled and dined all across the kingdom. The little mermaid's eyes filled with love every time she looked at the prince, but he never saw the true meaning in her gaze.

One day, the prince summoned the little mermaid to his chamber.

"I have news," he said, frowning. "It is time for me to marry. I must voyage to meet the princess of a foreign land. My parents insist that I marry her, although I don't have the heart for it."

The little mermaid's eyes filled with hope. She reached for the prince's hand.

"I can't marry this princess," he confessed, "I have another, secret, love. Once a girl saved me from drowning. She was kind and beautiful, just like you. I know I will never find her, but she is the only person that I could ever truly love."

The prince's words seared through the little mermaid's heart. She remembered the morning after the shipwreck. She could still feel the pain of hiding amongst the waves, watching the prince lying on the sand. The little mermaid wished that she could tell him the truth – that she was his true rescuer, not the girl that he'd smiled upon! Instead she could do nothing. With a heavy heart, the little mermaid helped the prince prepare for his journey.

When the prince's galleon landed in the foreign port, the whole kingdom turned out to greet him. Trumpets played, horses pranced and courtiers lined the beaches. At the very end of the pier, the princess was waiting.

"Greetings, Your Majesty," smiled the prince, dropping to one knee.

The little mermaid gasped in surprise. She had seen the princess's face before. It was the girl who had run down onto the beach on the fateful day after the storm! She looked more beautiful than the little mermaid had remembered. The princess had tumbling blonde hair, rosebud lips and shimmering blue eyes.

The prince took the princess in his arms and twirled her round and round.

"It was you!" he declared. "You are the girl that saved me! Without you I would still be lying at the bottom of the sea. My dream has come true!"

The little mermaid felt her heart break. As she tiptoed away, she heard the prince proposing to his new love. Church bells pealed in celebration.

The wedding was spectacular. The prince and princess sealed their marriage on board the royal ship. The little mermaid watched silently as the bride and groom made their vows on the top deck, surrounded by their family and friends.

The bride looked radiant. The groom's coal-black eyes glittered just like they did on the little mermaid's first night above the surface.

"And now it is my very last night," thought the little mermaid. "Soon I will disappear into nothing, like the foam on the sea."

"Wait! There is hope!" cried a voice.

The little mermaid ran to the side of the ship and looked overboard. She saw her five sisters lifting their heads out of the water. Their beautiful tresses had been cut jagged and short.

"We have given our hair to the sea witch," explained the eldest princess, holding out a glistening dagger. "In return she gave us this knife. Use it to kill the prince and the spell will be broken. You can come home and be a mermaid once more."

The little mermaid's eyes welled up with grateful tears. She took the knife and ran towards the prince's cabin. But when she stood outside, she could not even bring herself to knock on the door. The little mermaid thought of the prince's dear face and realised that she

could never do him harm. Instead she flung the knife overboard, far out into the ocean. The waves around it turned blood red as it sank down into the shadows.

The little mermaid had too much love for the prince in her heart. When the dawn came, she closed her eyes and leapt from the ship into the water below as the morning sun touched the surface. But just as she thought that she was turning into foam, hundreds of melodious voices started crying through the surf.

"Come with us. Come with us!"

The little mermaid suddenly felt herself rising upwards. A host of golden air spirits encircled her, then joined together in a beautiful embrace.

"We are the daughters of the air," they sang. "We are devoted to helping others. Pure spirits like ours cannot die, and good deeds and kindness will give us immortal souls one day. Your heart is just as selfless, just as true. You belong with us, little mermaid. Rise up and feel the warmth of the sunshine."

A peace came over the little mermaid. Down below her, the prince and his bride stood on the deck, gazing out across the ocean.

"Goodbye, my love," she smiled. "Be happy."

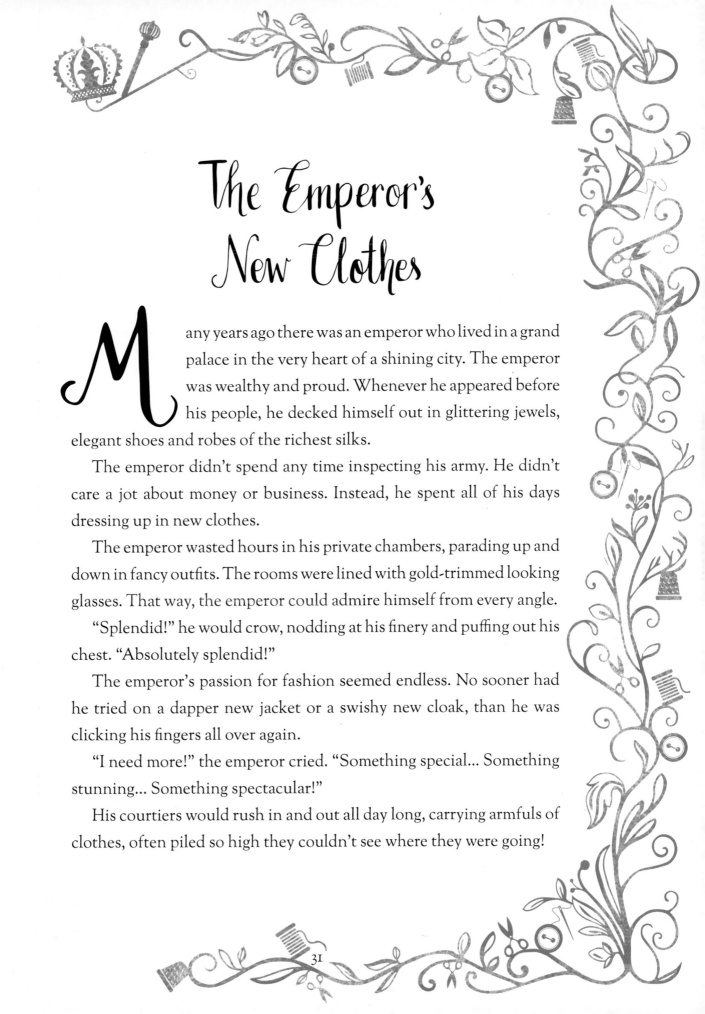

The Emperor's New Clothes

Many years ago there was an emperor who lived in a grand palace in the very heart of a shining city. The emperor was wealthy and proud. Whenever he appeared before his people, he decked himself out in glittering jewels, elegant shoes and robes of the richest silks.

The emperor didn't spend any time inspecting his army. He didn't care a jot about money or business. Instead, he spent all of his days dressing up in new clothes.

The emperor wasted hours in his private chambers, parading up and down in fancy outfits. The rooms were lined with gold-trimmed looking glasses. That way, the emperor could admire himself from every angle.

"Splendid!" he would crow, nodding at his finery and puffing out his chest. "Absolutely splendid!"

The emperor's passion for fashion seemed endless. No sooner had he tried on a dapper new jacket or a swishy new cloak, than he was clicking his fingers all over again.

"I need more!" the emperor cried. "Something special... Something stunning... Something spectacular!"

His courtiers would rush in and out all day long, carrying armfuls of clothes, often piled so high they couldn't see where they were going!

Before long, the emperor's closets were overflowing. The palace buzzed with tailors, seamstresses and hat makers, working night and day. There was always something new for them to make – the emperor never wore the same outfit twice!

Every morning, the prime minister was summoned to the emperor's dressing room. He would be told to sit and wait while His Majesty got dressed. Courtiers swarmed around the emperor, polishing belt buckles and fastening ties.

"Look at me today!" the emperor would finally say, stepping out in his latest look. "Aren't I the best-dressed emperor in the whole wide world?"

The prime minister would cough politely, and then sink into a deep bow. His answer was always the same:

"Yes, Your Majesty. You most certainly are."

The emperor's extravagant tastes soon became famous far and wide. Merchants came to the city, hoping to sell him clothes, jewellery and shoes. But even their finest wares didn't satisfy the emperor for long.

One morning, two strangers appeared at the palace gates. Between them they carried an enormous trunk with a padlock on the front.

"Who goes there?" demanded the gatekeepers.

"We require an audience with the emperor," they said boldly.

The gatekeepers eyed the pair suspiciously. One man was tall and gangly, with eyes that darted left and right. The other was a small, round fellow squeezed into a waistcoat that was straining at the buttons.

"We are master-weavers," declared the tall man. "We make robes that are fit for kings!"

At that moment, the prime minister scurried past carrying an armful of official papers and decrees.

"The emperor doesn't see anyone unless they have an appointment," he called over his shoulder, without even a backwards glance.

"He will want to see *us*," the man called after him. "Our weaving is the talk of royalty! We only make clothes for the greatest rulers in the world."

"And what clothing it is!" chipped in his friend. "Words can't describe such luxury. Our colours and patterns will take your breath away. Every thread is a masterpiece!"

The prime minister stopped. There was a royal procession through the city the very next week. Once a year the emperor paraded before his people – and he expected every subject to line the streets and cheer.

The emperor had spent months trying to pick the perfect outfit to wear, but still hadn't found one special enough. Maybe these weavers could conjure up a creation that would please him? The costume would need to be unique and the most stupendous thing the emperor had ever seen.

The prime minister turned on his heel. He flashed his friendliest smile.

"Gentlemen," he said. "Do come this way..."

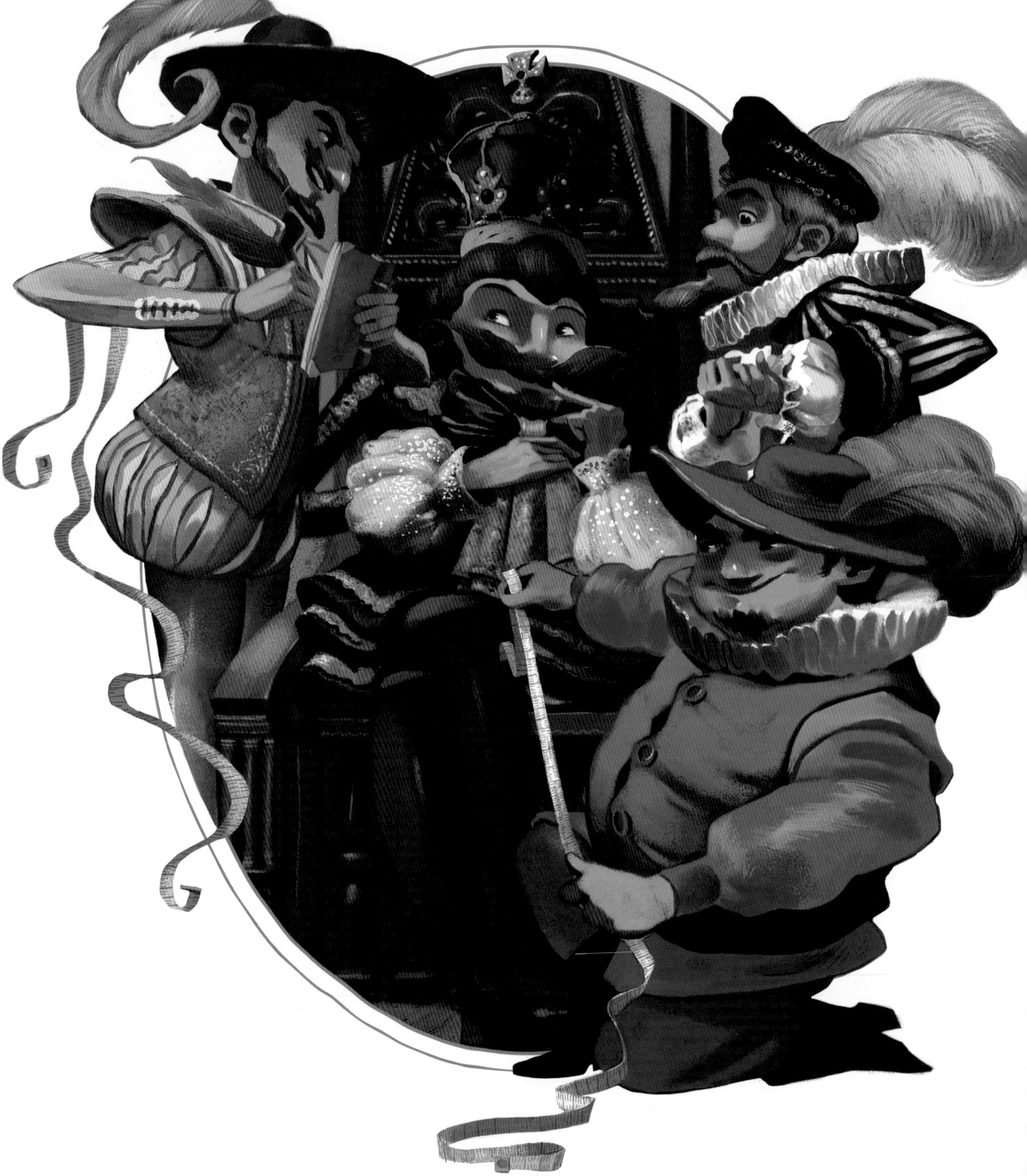

The emperor was delighted to meet these men who claimed to be master-weavers. He listened carefully as they explained their craft.

"Our designs are exceptional," insisted the weavers. "No two pieces are the same! Each is created from the rarest fabric. It is lighter than gossamer, more sheer than silk! The garments slip on with such ease, it is almost as if you are wearing nothing at all."

The prime minister bowed graciously.

"Perhaps this might be something Your Majesty would like to consider for the royal procession?" he murmured.

The emperor's eyes lit up at once.

"Yes! Of course, I would need a design that is... exclusive," he said pompously. "Robes that are befitting of a great emperor. No expense could be spared."

The weavers rubbed their chins. For a moment, the prime minister fancied that he saw a little wink pass between them, but when he looked again they were busily pulling out quills and tape measures.

"We will stitch something spectacular for His Highness," said the tall weaver. "It shall fit like a glove! Of course the crowds will flock around you, but only the lucky few will be able to enjoy the true marvel of our creation. Your Majesty will be the talk of the kingdom!"

"Only the lucky few?" asked the emperor.

The small, round weaver's voice faded into a whisper.

"We design for the richest and most powerful people on the world," he boasted. "Our pieces aren't worn by any old riff-raff. Indeed, our fabrics are so refined, only the cleverest and most sophisticated people can even *see* them."

The tall weaver looked straight at the prime minister and said, "To anyone else – they're simply invisible. It's like there's nothing there at all!"

"Anyone stupid, unworthy or vulgar won't be able to see our cloth," smirked the small, round weaver. "It's quite simple, really."

The prime minister started to protest at the idea, but the emperor silenced him with a wave of his hand. The weavers' proposition sounded fascinating! Once he was wearing these fine new robes, the emperor would be able to tell who truly deserved their place in his court. He could dismiss all of the dull, lazy people and surround himself only with those cultured enough to deserve his company.

The emperor jumped to his feet, then pulled on a scarlet cord hanging next to his throne. A bell rang out across the palace.

"Summon the treasurer!" he declared. "I want to make a royal commission."

The deal was soon struck. The treasurer trudged down to the palace dungeons and unlocked the royal vault. Twelve footmen were sent marching back up to the throne room, each carrying a bag of gold coins.

"That will do nicely," nodded the weavers, sharing the bags out between them.

"Prime minister," ordered the emperor. "Find an empty chamber for our visitors and set up a loom for them to work on. Give them everything they need. They have a very important job to do."

The prime minister nodded politely, then led the weavers away. He noticed that the men were both grinning from ear to ear.

The prime minister wondered if he had done the right thing introducing this pair to the emperor, who was so easily taken in. It sounded impossible for the weavers to be able to make clothes invisible to foolish people! But it was too late now. The emperor's new clothes would be the talk of the kingdom in no time at all. Nobody would be able to wait to see the emperor's fine robes! Who would be worthy enough to admire them? Who wouldn't be able to see them at all?

The weavers had just one week to create their masterpiece.

"We will need materials to work with," announced the tall weaver. "Bring us gold thread, silks and precious gems in every colour and shade."

The prime minister wrote a list, then sent the footmen out to order what was needed. When the goods arrived, the weavers made a great show of inspecting every item. They pored over each roll of silk, picking out only the costliest fabric. Golden thread was teased and pulled. Rubies and pearls, diamonds and sapphires were held up to the light.

"Yes," decided the weavers, packing everything into their enormous trunk. "These will do. Now leave us. It is time to weave."

When the prime minister closed the chamber door, the men bolted it behind him.

"What are they up to?" he muttered.

The weavers appeared to toil by sunlight and candlelight, never leaving the locked room. The loom clack-clacked as they worked and scissors snip-snipped. Entry to the chamber was strictly forbidden. No one would be allowed in until it was time to unveil the outfit for the royal procession. The emperor tried to be patient, but he was not used to waiting for anything. He soon became anxious and fidgety, calling the prime minister to his private dressing room.

"The day of the procession will be here before we know it," the emperor said, pacing up and down. "I need to know all is in hand."

"I understand of course, Your Majesty," soothed the prime minister. "The weavers do seem very busy…"

"But I don't even know what colour I will be wearing!" exclaimed the emperor. "This can't do. It can't do at all."

The prime minister nodded. "Shall I escort you to the weavers' chamber?" he asked. "Your Majesty can inspect the fabric for himself."

The emperor shook his head. Something about the weavers' promise made him nervous. What if he, the world's best-dressed emperor, could not see their fantastic threads? That would make him foolish. So the emperor sent the prime minister along instead to test whether he was worthy of his position.

"I am far too busy for such errands," the emperor sniffed, as the prime minister trooped out of the door.

The prime minister knocked on the weavers' door.

"His Majesty has asked me to inspect your work," he said. "Everything must be perfect for the royal procession, you understand."

To the prime minister's surprise, the two men welcomed him inside. He expected to see a chamber strewn with mannequins, patterns and thread. Instead there was nothing. The loom stood empty in the middle of the room.

"We are exhausted," said the small weaver, pulling a handkerchief out of his waistcoat pocket and mopping his brow. "The loom has been running day and night!"

"Has it?" spluttered the prime minister.

The tall weaver looked affronted.

"Of course," he replied, stretching out his arms even though he wasn't holding anything. "How else do you think we made this?"

"Look at the fabric we have created for His Majesty," said the small weaver, pointing at thin air. "Isn't it divine?"

The prime minister's heart sank. Even when he got up close, he couldn't spot a single thing! The weavers pointed and admired every aspect of the cloth, urging the prime minister to join in.

"I must be a fool!" he muttered to himself.

"So tell us," said the weavers. "What do you think?"

The prime minister took a deep breath. He thought about the emperor, waiting upstairs. He thought about the royal procession. He made a decision.

"It is a triumph," he lied. "Such artistry! I've never seen cloth like it! I shall be sure to tell the emperor what I have seen. Thank you, gentlemen. Please get back to your work."

The weavers pretended to roll up the invisible cloth.

"Just one thing before you go," said the small weaver.

"Ah, yes..." smiled his friend. "We are running out of materials. A costume of this size is very intricate, you see. We need more silk, more thread and more jewels. Yes, we definitely need more jewels!"

"There's our wages, too," added the small, round weaver. "There is still much for us to do. We will require twelve more bags of gold if we are to finish everything to the high standard that His Majesty expects."

The emperor was trying on hats when the prime minister returned.

"So?" he demanded. "How am I going to look on procession day?"

The prime minister paused, but then he said, "Stunning. Spectacular, Your Majesty! The cloth is truly unique."

The emperor clapped his hands. He made the prime minister describe every detail of the wonderful new clothes – the cut of every seam, every colour and every pattern. The weavers' work sounded so splendid, he was happy to grant their request for more money.

"Send the treasurer along with all of the gold that they need," he ordered. "And tell him to report back what *he* thinks of my new robes."

The treasurer had the gold brought up to the master-weavers' chamber. The emperor had always had expensive tastes, but even he had never spent so much on just one outfit.

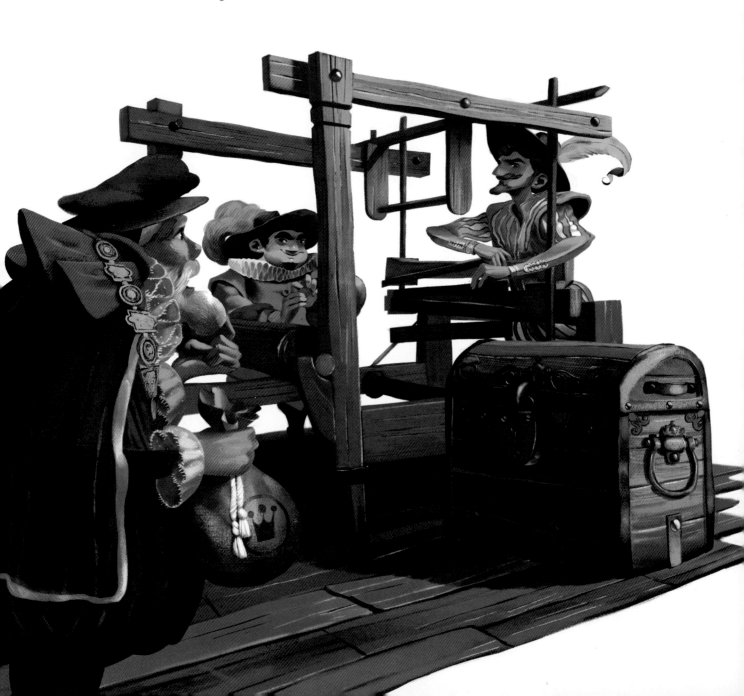

"This cloth had better be good," he grumbled. "We'll need to raise taxes at this rate."

The treasurer had worked at the palace ever since he was a young boy. The emperor trusted him almost as much as the prime minister. But when the treasurer went inside, he was in for a dreadful shock. He couldn't see anything, either! To him, the weavers' loom looked completely empty. There wasn't a single thread in sight.

"Can it be that I'm unfit to serve the emperor?" worried the treasurer. After all his years of service, he could not bear the thought of anyone knowing such a terrible secret. The treasurer did what the prime minister had done before him. He lied.

"May I take this opportunity to congratulate you both," praised the treasurer. "The emperor will be enchanted."

The treasurer scuttled straight to the emperor and passed on the lie. His Majesty was thrilled, but more than a little nervous. He hoped that he would see the wonderful new clothes, just as his officials did!

The day of the royal procession grew closer and the sense of expectation could be felt by everyone in the kingdom. Jugglers and jesters performed in the streets and flags flew outside the houses. Visitors from far and wide streamed into the city. Everybody wanted to see the emperor step out in his magnificent new clothes.

On the night before the grand event, the loom in the weavers' chamber clack-clacked non-stop until dawn. As soon as the sun rose, the pair unbolted the door. They made their way up to the emperor's private chambers.

The emperor sat in his dressing room, wearing only his finest silk underwear. His hair was styled, his teeth had been cleaned and his nails had been polished to perfection. Now he just needed to get dressed.

The weavers made their entrance. The prime minister, the treasurer and all the emperor's most trusted advisors followed them inside.

"Your Majesty," said the tall weaver. "We present your new clothes."

The small weaver stepped forward, with his arms outstretched.

"This is your shirt," he said solemnly. "May I help you put it on?"

The tall weaver pinched his forefingers and thumbs together. "And these are Your Majesty's breeches," he added proudly.

The emperor made a startled squeak. To him, it looked as if the weavers weren't holding anything at all! He eyed them both as closely as he dared, but the cloth was utterly invisible.

This was nothing short of a disaster.

The emperor looked to his advisors. The prime minister was gasping in admiration. The treasurer's face was stretched into a wide grin.

"I'm not fit to wear my crown!" thought the emperor. "What a scandal! No one can ever know – the kingdom would fall into chaos."

The weavers continued to pretend to help the emperor into his new clothes.

"Don't forget the flowing cloak," the small weaver said with a knowing chuckle.

His friend moved over to the ornate mirror in the corner of the dressing room.

"So," the tall weaver said, rubbing his hands together. "What does Your Majesty think?"

"I think," started the emperor, "I look very... elegant. The cloth feels as smooth and as light as a feather."

The weavers bowed, their eyes dancing with glee. The emperor stood still while they fussed and flapped around him, adjusting pretend buttons, straightening pretend collars and tying pretend bows.

"Your Majesty is now officially ready," announced the tall weaver.

With that, the whole room burst into a round of applause.

"May I be the first to say," praised the prime minister, "that the colour suits you to perfection."

"And the style," added the treasurer. "It is sublime. What a sumptuous outfit! Today, you are truly without equal!"

Everybody agreed, convincing the emperor that he had to be the only fool in the room. He was too proud to admit he couldn't see the clothes, so he carried on.

"Thank you," he said grandly, turning to the weavers. "From now on you will be known as the 'Royal Master-Weavers'."

It was time for the royal procession to begin. The emperor gathered his invisible robes and swept down the palace stairs. Footmen and chambermaids hid their shock when they saw him striding by in just his underwear!

The royal butler placed a crown upon the emperor's head, then passed him his golden sceptre. The palace gates were opened. The emperor puffed out his chest and stepped out into the sunshine.

The procession was a magnificent sight. Gleaming white horses pranced in rows, their bridles decorated with purple plumes. There were canopies fringed with gold and red, trumpet players and marching soldiers.

The only people not lining the streets were the weavers, who had sneaked away, taking their trunk filled with the emperor's treasures.

"Look!" cried a voice. "There's the emperor."

For just one second, the crowd went silent. Then they cheered.

"Look at his cloak," they marvelled. "How it glitters in the sunlight."

"You can tell he has the finest clothes in the world," they chattered. "What a perfect fit!"

Everybody pretended that they could see the new clothes. Nobody wanted to look stupid or vulgar.

The emperor straightened his back, thrilled by the applause.

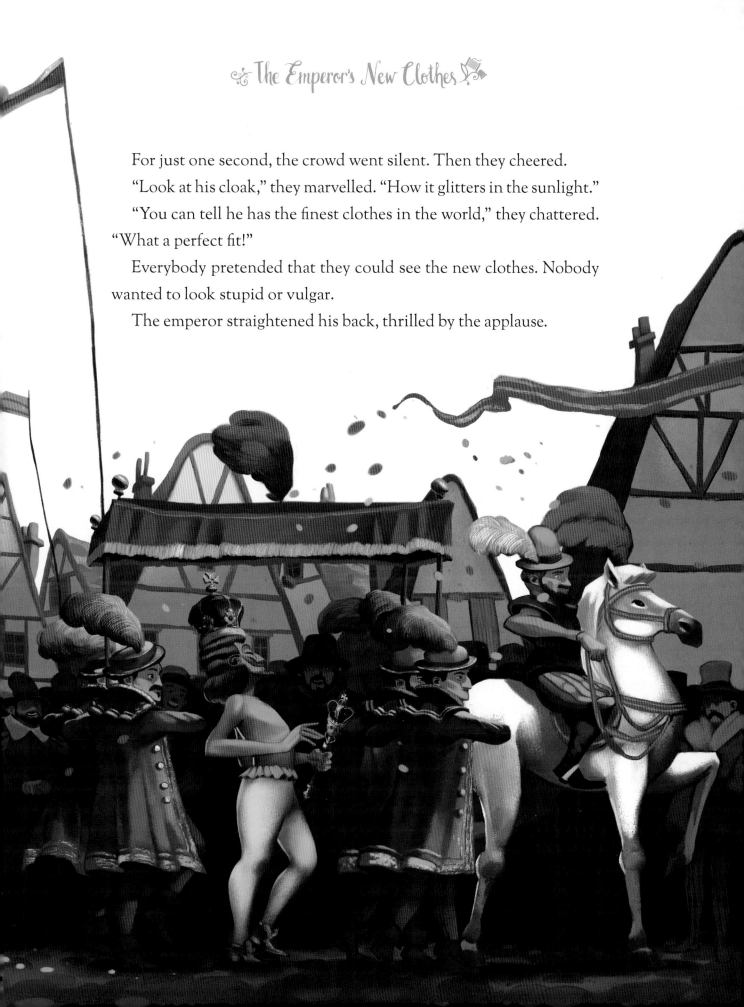

Just then a little child found his way to the front. He tugged on his father's hand.

"What are they saying?" he asked innocently. "I can't see any clothes at all!"

The little boy's father tried to pretend that it was all a game, but still he carried on.

"The emperor hasn't got any clothes on. Has he, Daddy?"

"Did you ever hear such innocent talk?" said the father to the surrounding crowd.

At first, people were shocked by the child's claim. Then they started to nudge each other and repeat what the boy had said. Suddenly the crowd burst into hoots of laughter as they realised the truth.

"The emperor hasn't got anything on!" they cried, whooping at the sight.

The prime minister and treasurer didn't know what to do. The emperor gulped, because he realised the crowd was right. The weavers had tricked him, and now he was parading before the entire kingdom in only his underwear! But he didn't stop or demand any real clothes to cover himself. He was too proud to admit that he'd been fooled.

"The procession must go on," he told himself. And he walked more proudly than ever in the clothes that weren't there at all.

The Ugly Duckling

Summer had come to the farm. Bumblebees buzzed in and out of the hedgerows, and buttercups turned up their merry yellow faces. Out in the fields, rows of golden wheat swayed and rippled in the breeze. The cows grazed lazily in the orchard, strolling past trees bent low with apples and sticky, sweet plums.

In a sleepy corner of the farm, tucked away behind an old barn, there was a dandelion patch. The patch was sheltered from the wind by a leafy bush. A cosy nest was tucked away there, right in the middle, and a plump mother duck sat on the nest, waiting for her eggs to hatch.

"How much longer will it be?" she asked herself for the hundredth time already that morning.

The mother duck had sat on the nest for weeks. She had tried hard to be patient, but it wasn't easy sitting by herself for hours on end. Whenever the other ducks waddled down to the river, she quacked at them and waggled her tail feathers. Sometimes the passers-by could be persuaded to stop for a word or two, but they were soon on their way. No duck wanted to waste the day gossiping in a dandelion patch when they could be paddling down the river instead!

Today, however, the mother duck was in luck. Her wait was finally over. The eggs were ready to hatch.

Tap-tap-tap!

The mother duck jumped up from her nest and pushed at the straw with her beak. Six creamy white eggs began to wobble and shake.

Tap-tap-tap!

"Come over here! Quick!" called the mother duck, spotting three friends waddling down for their morning swim. "My babies are coming!"

The ducks gathered round the nest. One by one the eggs began to crack and split. Then out popped a duckling with fuzzy yellow feathers.

"Ahhh!" cooed the ducks. "What a gorgeous little fellow he is!"

With that, another duckling appeared... and then another... and another! Soon the mother duck had six babies to call her own. The ducklings tumbled out of their shells, cheeping sweetly and blinking up at the daylight.

"A beautiful brood!" declared the other ducks, nodding their heads in approval.

The mother duck puffed her feathers out in pride. The little chicks were even more adorable than she'd imagined they'd be! Each one was the colour of sunshine, with bright eyes and tiny pink feet.

"Dear little ducklings," said the mother duck. "Are you all here?"

She nudged the hay around the nest. One last egg peeped out of the straw. It was the biggest of the lot.

"Still not hatched!" she quacked. "How much longer are you going to be? There's nothing else for it, I suppose. I'll have to sit back down and keep waiting."

The mother duck couldn't help but feel cross as she watched the other chicks pecking and playing. When would this last one hatch?

She couldn't wait to take her brood up to the farmyard to show them off to the other animals. How they would cluck when they saw their little yellow feathers and pretty little feet!

An old white duck wandered up, then tapped the last egg with her beak.

"That's no duckling you've got there," said the white duck.

The mother duck's feathers started to ruffle, but the visitor carried on.

"That's a turkey egg," she announced. "Mark my words! I was taken in once, just like you. I turned my back for five minutes and a great thing like that rolled into the nest. Ugh! It hatched into the ugliest turkey you've ever seen!"

"But that can't be," protested the mother duck. "I've been sat here for weeks!"

The white duck sniffed. "That's as maybe. All I'll say is that I know a turkey egg when I see it! Push it out and get on with looking after the rest of your chicks."

The other visitors hooted and quacked their agreement, putting the mother duck into a dreadful fluster. She peered down at the last egg. It looked so lonely, lying there all by itself. Who knew what would become of it if she upped and left?

"I won't leave it," she decided, settling herself back down on her nest. "I've waited this long. A few more days will make no difference." Another day and another night passed. The mother duck waited and waited for the last egg to hatch.

Tap-tap-tap!

The mother duck tipped her head to one side. At last! A crack zigzagged down the egg. It suddenly split in half, sending a duckling tumbling out into the nest. The mother duck carefully looked it up and down.

The duckling blinked at his mother. He wasn't tiny, yellow or cute. He was big and grey with a funny black beak.

"Oh dear," she frowned. "You're very odd, aren't you? You must have been stuck in that egg for too long. What dowdy feathers! And what enormous feet!"

The mother duck's friends came up to meet the new arrival.

"Peep-peep," said the duckling, as sweetly as he could.

"Are you sure it's not a turkey chick instead?" laughed the old white duck that had visited the day before.

The haughty brown duck from a nearby nest began to chuckle to herself.

"I do declare," she said loudly, "that he's the ugliest thing I've ever seen!"

"What a strange creature," said a drake, nudging the baby with his beak. "He doesn't look like a duckling at all!"

The mother duck wouldn't listen to another word. She tucked the newborn under her wing, then shooed the visitors away.

"Leave him alone," she quacked. "How can a baby be ugly? He's not good-looking yet, but I dare say he'll grow handsome. Just you wait!"

The other ducks waddled off, hooting and laughing as they went.

The mother duck sighed. Six perfect yellow babies and now this! Soon the whole farmyard would be talking about her poor ugly duckling. What was she to do?

The mother duck waited for the sun to climb up above the barn roof. When the afternoon breeze felt warm on her feathers, she led her little family down to the riverbank. Six yellow chicks bounced along behind her in a neat line. The last grey duckling tagged along at the back, stumbling through the grass and tripping over his big webbed feet.

The mother duck's heart fluttered at the thought of leading her brood. At the river, she slid elegantly into the water.

"Follow me, children," she said. "Do what I do."

Plop! Plop! Plop! The six little chicks jumped in. The babies squealed and cheeped with delight when they felt the cool water tickling their tummies. Without even thinking, they pushed their heads up, kicked their legs and paddled.

PLOP! The ugly duckling jumped in, too. To the mother duck's delight, he began to paddle along just as beautifully as his siblings.

"That's my boy!" she told herself proudly. "What turkey can swim like that? Look at his straight neck and those strong legs. He's a fine little swimmer!"

The mother duck was so pleased, she resolved to forget about the other silly ducks. Her grey duckling was a bit large and rather plain, but she was certain that was just because he had stayed in his egg too long. A few days of sunshine on his feathers was all he needed to make him just as handsome as the rest.

"This way, ducklings!" she called, jumping back onto the riverbank. Now that she was confident that her youngest couldn't be a turkey, the mother duck decided to take the chicks up to the farmyard. She was ready to show them off to the other animals.

"And what do we have here?" asked the old horse, ambling over as soon as he spotted the mother duck waddling into the farmyard. He counted six cheeping chicks behind her, followed by a funny creature with a dull black beak. The cows, the goats and the hens all rushed over to get a better look.

The mother duck puffed her chest out.

"These are my new arrivals," she said loudly.

The horse whinnied in surprise. The chicks were delightful of course, but what was this drab grey bird following at the end of the line? He asked the little creature to step forward.

"Head up straight, turn your toes out!" whispered the mother duck, nudging the grey duckling with her beak.

The grey duckling gulped nervously. He waddled clumsily to the front, then peered up at the farm animals.

"Hello," he said, in a shy voice.

"Oh my!" squawked the hen. "What kind of bird is that? He hasn't hatched at all well. If only you could put him back in his egg! How disappointed I'd be if I had a chick like that."

The mother duckling glared at the hen.

"He's just a little different, that's all," she retorted angrily. "You should see how well he swims!"

But everyone had stopped listening to the mother duck. The farm animals were too busy shouting and laughing.

"He's twice the size he ought to be!" neighed the horse.

"And so ugly!" mooed the cow.

"He certainly doesn't belong here!" bleated the goat, pointing his horns at the ugly duckling.

"Just give him time," insisted the mother duck, shooing her brood back towards the nest. "He'll grow into a handsome drake one day!"

But that just made the farm animals hoot even louder than before.

From that moment on, the ugly duckling was sad and lonely. Every time he strayed into the farmyard, the animals turned their backs on him. On some days, children wandered over to feed the ducks. They cooed and squealed when they spotted the six fluffy chicks, but they wouldn't throw any food to the grey bird with the horrible black feet. When the ducklings went to the river, the six pretty chicks paddled off in a line, leaving the ugly duckling to swim all by himself.

"What am I to do with you?" muttered the mother duck, looking him sadly up and down. "You've caused me nothing but trouble ever since you hatched!"

The ugly duckling's eyes welled up with tears. Even his own mother didn't seem to want him anymore!

"I should just swim away," he decided. "They'd be better off without me."

The poor ugly duckling paddled downstream. As he swam, all he could see was his gloomy reflection in the water – a mass of drab grey feathers and a gawky black beak.

Far behind him, the mother duck led her chicks out of the water, not even noticing that her youngest had disappeared.

"This way, children," she called. "Follow me."

The ugly duckling kicked his legs as hard as he could, pressing on even faster. Soon the barn and the dandelion patch were far behind him. The river turned into a meandering stream weaving in and out of the meadows.

After a while, the sun began to set. The ugly duckling flew up out of the stream, hoping to seek out shelter and some company. The birds living in the trees and hedgerows darted away the very instant the stranger came near. Rabbits hopped back into their burrows and chattering squirrels pointed down rudely from their branches. Even the wild ducks eyed him suspiciously.

"What a strange thing you are!" they quacked, shrinking back from the ugly duckling. "You can't mix with us. Understand?"

The ugly duckling nodded miserably. He tucked himself in amongst a pile of leaves and hid until daybreak.

Early next morning, the ugly duckling got on his way. He waddled through the forest until he reached a glassy lake surrounded by bulrushes. A flock of geese were diving for grubs and worms.

"They're huge!" the ugly duckling whispered to himself.

The geese honked noisily as they ate. The ugly duckling summoned up all of his courage, then jumped down to the edge of the lake.

"Hello there!" he called out bravely. "Have you seen any ducklings that look like me?"

A white goose shook his head in surprise, spraying water everywhere.

"Like you?" he spluttered, turning to his friends. "Why you're the strangest looking duckling I've ever seen!"

The other geese hooted at the thought. Their answer was clear – the ugly duckling certainly didn't belong with them.

The ugly duckling bowed his head sadly and left the lake. He stumbled on through marshlands and meadow, up steep hills and down winding valley paths. Walking was difficult and slow. The ugly duckling was still just a chick, even if he wasn't fluffy and cute.

"It's getting cold," sighed the ugly duckling, watching the trees arch and bend in the breeze. Clouds began to swirl overhead. The sky turned slate grey and rain began to fall. The little bird was buffeted left and right, but he kept on going until it got late.

Just as he was about to faint with tiredness, the ugly duckling spotted an old cottage looming out of the shadows. It had holes in the roof and a creaky wooden door that swung from a rusted hinge. The garden hadn't been tended for years and weeds sprouted across the path. Despite this, a light shone from the window.

"The storm is almost here," he whispered to himself. "I'll have to take my chances."

The ugly duckling rushed forward, pushing his head down against the driving rain. He waddled up the garden path, jumping in and out of the puddles. When a gust of wind blew the cottage door open a crack, the ugly duckling crept inside.

The cottage only had one room. There were no fusses or frills, but it was dry and warm enough. An old woman was sitting in front of the fire, dozing in her rocking chair. There was a fine grey cat curled up on her lap. In the corner, there was a nest of hay with a plump hen perched on top. The ugly duckling hid under the table so that no one would see him.

"How's my beautiful chicky?" asked the woman, waking herself up to stoke the fire.

The hen lifted herself grandly off her nest. There, underneath, was a newly laid speckled egg. The woman picked it up, patted the hen, then gave the cat a kiss for good measure.

"Well done!" she beamed. "What a lucky woman I am! Fresh eggs every day from my prize hen and a handsome cat for company! I couldn't wish for anything more."

The cat purred contentedly and stretched his paws out so his mistress could stroke him, arching his back as she brushed his fur backwards and forwards.

"What a generous lady," marvelled the ugly duckling. "I wonder what she will think of me?"

The poor little bird leant back against the table leg. He was so weary, he dropped off to sleep instantly, safe at last from the wind and rain.

"And who might you be?" bellowed a voice.

The ugly duckling's eyes sprang open. Daylight streamed into the cottage. The old woman, the cat and the hen were all squeezed under the table, looking him up and down!

The ugly duckling cleared his throat and flapped to his feet.

"Hello," he said as politely as he could. "I am a duckling."

The cat snorted. The hen squawked. There was no room for strangers in their house!

"Hmm," said the old woman, thinking for a moment. She fancied the idea of having duck eggs as well as chicken eggs for breakfast every day. "Let's give the duckling a try," she said to the cat and the hen. "If it can lay me lots of eggs, it can stay."

The ugly duckling gasped in surprise. It was a relief to have somewhere to shelter, but he knew it could not last for long. He was a drake – a male duck – and drakes do not lay eggs.

"Can you lay eggs that are as big and round as mine?" demanded the hen one afternoon, fluffing up her feathers.

"No," sighed the ugly duckling. "I cannot."

"Can you purr and arch your back?" hissed the cat, swishing his tail left and right.

"No," sighed the ugly duckling. "I cannot."

There was nothing more to say. The cat and the hen watched as the ugly duckling waddled back outside to face the big wide world.

The ugly duckling roamed on and on, but now there was a slight chill in the air. Autumn was coming. Soon there would be swirls of russet and gold as the leaves changed colour, then let go of their branches.

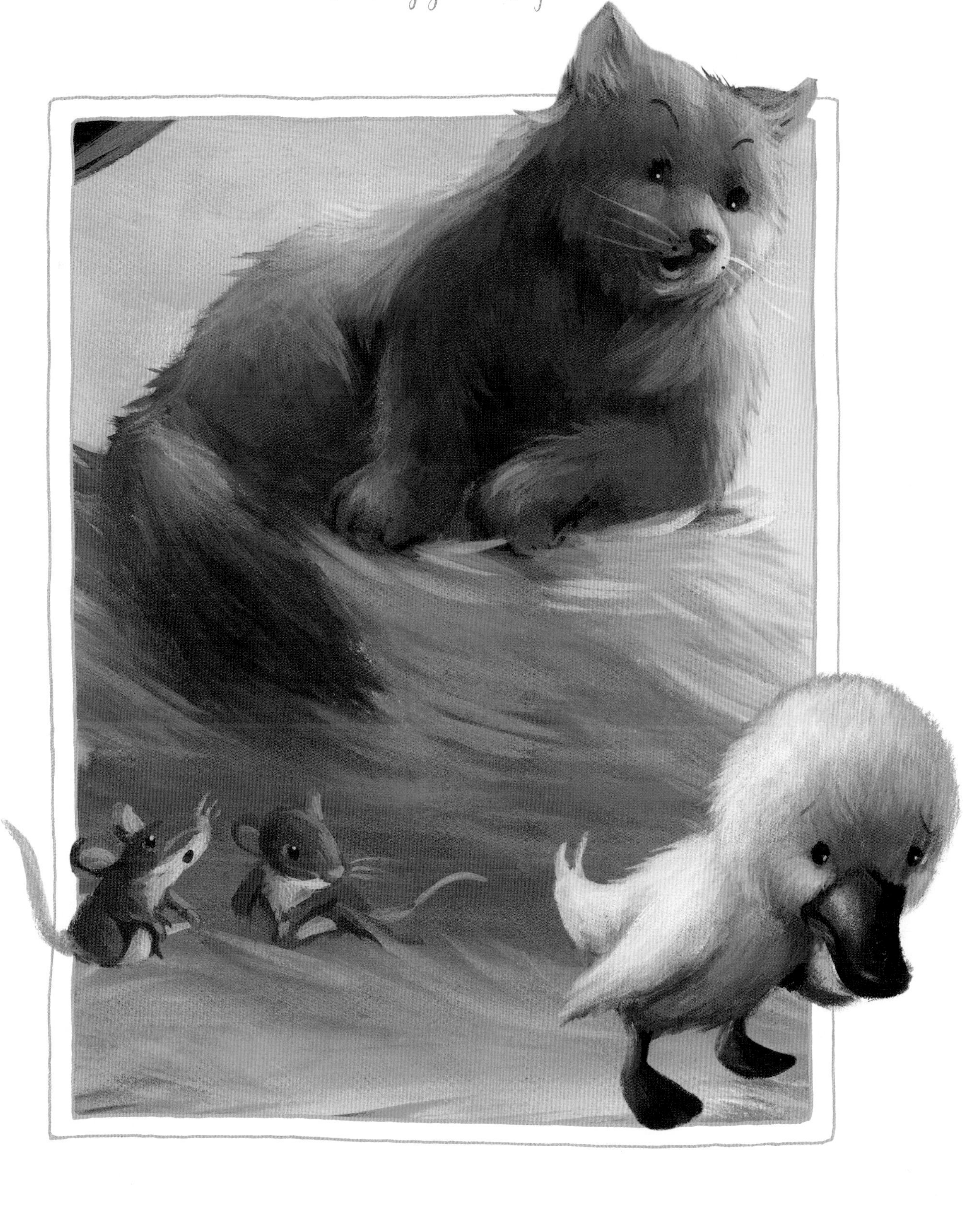

The ugly duckling called out to the birds and the animals that he passed, but nobody wanted to share their nest with a dowdy grey chick.

At last the ugly duckling stumbled across a big round pond, tucked away in the middle of a lonely wood. It was quiet here, apart from the frogs and fishes. The duckling shivered, then jumped into the water.

"Nobody wants me," he sniffed sadly. "I'll just have to hide here until the winter has passed."

It was a lonely life for a young duckling. Every day he paddled round the pond, searching for grubs and pondweed to nibble. Whenever another creature came down to the water, he rushed into the reeds and hid himself from view. Sometimes a frog would hop past and spy him first, then ribbet loudly in surprise.

"What an odd-looking duckling," he would croak. "Wait till I tell my friends!"

As he scrambled to cover himself with reeds, the ugly duckling would feel more and more ashamed. He shivered at the thought of the other animals laughing at him.

As the days grew colder, the ugly duckling stayed hidden in the reeds more and more. He sat in a clump of leaves, gazing up at the wide open sky above him.

One evening, just as the sun was setting, a flock of gleaming white birds flew overhead. The ugly duckling gasped at their beauty. Each bird had an elegant long neck, magnificent wings and feathers the colour of snow. They cried out as they flew, winging their way to spend the winter in warmer lands. Without thinking, the ugly duckling cried back – a strange, shrill shriek that cut through the icy air.

"They're the kings of the sky!" declared the ugly duckling, craning his head. He watched intently until every last bird had disappeared over the horizon.

"What beauty," gasped the ugly duckling. "If only I could look like them."

The chick lifted up a gawky grey wing, then sighed at his silliness. How could something so ugly dare to dream such an impossible dream?

It was a cold and miserable winter. The ugly duckling struggled to find food to eat in his lonely home. The pond froze over and the sky turned ashen and white. Then, one day, a lark began to sing a more hopeful tune. Spring was returning to the countryside!

The ugly duckling peered timidly out of the reeds. The pond was thawed now, and yellow irises opened their petals to the sun. Suddenly a graceful swan glided through the water, straight past the ugly duckling's hiding place.

"What are you doing here?" asked the swan, swimming closer.

The ugly duckling pulled his head back into the reeds. The swan was sure to be disgusted by the sight of such a drab, clumsy creature.

"I am sorry to offend you," he said sadly. "I'll get on my way..."

The swan glided right up to the ugly duckling.

"Why would you do that?" he asked. "Come on, the rest of us are waiting."

With that, three more noble white swans emerged from the other side of the pond. They curled their wing feathers up behind them so delicately, it made the ugly duckling hang his head

to be in the presence of such beauty. He stared down into the pond, then cried out in amazement. There in the water, was the reflection of a beautiful white swan, looking straight back up at him.

"Can that really be me?" he stuttered.

The other swans gathered around their new friend.

"Of course it is!" they replied, patting him gently with their beaks. "You are the youngest and most handsome of us all."

The ugly duckling felt tears of joy spring to his eyes. He arched his slender neck and set out across the water. The breeze felt warm as it ruffled through his feathers.

The beautiful swan had never dreamed of such happiness when he was the ugly duckling. He flapped his wings and rose up into the air with the other swans – ready to start a new, better life.

The Fir Tree

In the very heart of a beautiful forest, there stood a little fir tree. Although it was still young, the fir tree grew straight and true. Its trunk was strong and its branches were mossy green. The fir tree's boughs were studded with a hundred tiny fir cones, each no bigger than your thumb.

The tree stood on a pretty hillside. It had enough sunshine to warm its cones, but also shelter from the wind and rain. Fine trees towered all around it, standing side by side like brothers.

Every morning the sun rose from behind the mountains, lighting the forest in reds, pinks and golds. Flowers unfurled their petals, filling the air with sweet fragrance. Every afternoon little children would run in and out of the woods, picking wild strawberries. The hillside echoed with the sound of their laughter and songs.

Days like these should have made the fir tree feel contented, but it was impatient and dissatisfied. It didn't like being the smallest tree in the forest. Instead of enjoying the children's games, all the fir tree could think about was the day when it would be as big and strong as the trees standing beside it.

Sometimes, when they got tired of strawberry picking, the boys and girls would sit down beside the fir tree.

"What an adorable little tree!" one would cry. "How tiny he is!"

"He's the baby of the wood!" another would exclaim.

This sort of chatter made the fir tree feel very cross indeed. It was tired of being young – it wanted to be the tallest, straightest, most magnificent fir in the forest!

"How dare they talk about me like that," it would grumble to itself. "Soon I'll tower over those children. Just wait and see!"

So that's how the fir tree carried on – wishing the days away, one after the other. When summer passed to winter, flurries of snowflakes whirled all around. The fir tree found no joy in the glittering carpet of snow that appeared.

Sometimes a hare would frisk over the fir tree's roots, kicking its feet out with each playful hop.

"That tickles!" grumbled the fir tree. "Leave me alone."

Even when a robin redbreast sat on the tree's branches and began a cheery song its spirits could not be lifted.

"Be quiet," groused the fir tree. "Perch somewhere else."

The fir tree had no time for songbirds. It was too busy imagining itself reaching up to the sky far above. Every time it looked up at the grown-up trees, the fir tree would give another little sigh.

"What a feeling it must be to sway back and forth like they do," it would think. "How much longer until it's my turn to be big and strong?"

Every year, the fir tree grew taller. As its branches spread, two more winters passed.

In the spring, the tree looked down at its new growth. It still wasn't half as big as it felt it should be.

"Hurry up, branches. Grow, grow, grow!" it complained. "Why does it take so long?"

The fir tree stretched its boughs higher and higher, straining to keep up with its neighbours.

When the next autumn came, a group of woodcutters rode into the forest. The fir tree watched as the men worked in teams to fell the grown-up trees standing just beside it. Warning cries rang out as the mighty trunks crashed to the ground. As soon as a tree was down, the woodcutters trimmed off its branches and boughs.

"Oh my!" gasped the fir tree. "What are they doing?"

It was hard to believe that it wouldn't see its noble neighbours ever again. One by one their trunks were lifted onto carts and dragged away.

The fir tree wondered where the other trees had gone. When the winter snow melted and the days got warmer again, storks came to the hillside. The birds picked their way through the moss, squawking about faraway lands. The fir tree wanted to know all about their travels.

"I flew south across the ocean," said a bird with a fine orange bill. "I soared over many ships. They had masts of timber, tall and sturdy, just like the pines in this forest. Perhaps they once grew in a place like this?"

The fir tree was enthralled. It imagined itself as a mast on a magnificent galleon. It yearned to tower above the deck and look down on the sailors below.

"I wish I was mighty enough to go to sea," it declared. "What an adventure that must be!"

When the stork went away, the wind ruffled the fir tree's branches.

"You are still young," it murmured. "These days are precious. You will be old soon enough. Trust me. I have seen the seasons turn more times than I can remember!"

The fir tree listened for a moment, then shook its needles and shrugged the breeze away.

Day by day, month by month, year by year, the fir tree kept growing. It wasn't young any more. While it stood rooted to its same familiar spot, it began to notice other things happening around it.

Every year, after the first flurry of snowflakes, the woodcutters would troop back into the forest again. They walked in and out of the trees, eyeing up their tips and pointing at their needles. At this time of year the men ignored the giants of the hillside – they wanted the younger trees instead. They wielded their axes and chopped them down, taking care not to damage their outstretched boughs.

"Why have those trees been chosen?" wondered the fir tree. "That one over there isn't even as tall as I am!"

The woodcutters seemed to be searching for the bushiest, most handsome firs. Instead of stripping off their branches, the men carefully laid the felled trees on a horse-drawn cart, then towed them back down the forest track.

The fir tree was almost mad with curiosity.

"What is happening?" it demanded. "Will somebody tell me?"

The sparrows had the answer. They told the fir tree what they had seen at the end of the forest trail.

"It's Christmas-time," they chirped. "Those trees are off to town. Soon they'll each be placed in a room at the front of a grand house. They'll be covered in beautiful decorations. We see them every year!"

The fir tree was captivated. The birds talked of twinkling lights, the smell of cinnamon and pearly glass baubles. To be decorated for Christmas sounded like the greatest honour any tree could wish for!

A thrill of excitement rushed through the fir tree's branches. Christmas in the town sounded spectacular, but what happened to the trees afterwards?

"That is all we have seen," replied the sparrows.

From that moment on, the fir tree didn't yearn for a life at sea. It had a new ambition – to be crowned as a glorious Christmas tree, standing in splendour for everyone to see and admire!

"If only Christmas would come right now," it sighed. "I'm just as tall as the other trees that were taken. Am I not just as handsome, too?"

The fir tree could think of nothing else. Winter thawed into spring and spring bloomed into summer, but the fir tree barely noticed. Shy snowdrops were followed by a carpet of bluebells,

dainty cowslips and blushing briar rose. As the forest blossomed, the fir tree also stretched and grew. It was now both tall and handsome. Walkers, huntsmen and couples would all stop beside its branches.

"Look at this one," they would say, gazing at its perfect shape and glistening evergreen needles. "What a beauty!"

When Christmas came round the next year, the fir tree was the very first tree to be cut down. The woodcutter admired it, then swung his axe low.

The tree quivered in surprise. Instead of pleasure, the blow made it feel faint with pain! Suddenly it was sad to be leaving the forest home that it had known for all of its life.

"Stay calm," the fir tree told itself firmly as it was laid on the back of the woodcutter's cart. "Think about that warm drawing room. Think about those twinkling decorations! Think how wonderful that will be."

More and more trees were put on the cart. There was barely any room to breathe! The woodcutter clicked his tongue and his horse began to trot back down the forest track, pulling the cart behind it. The fir tree peeped out timidly through the stack of branches. The canopy of trees above gave way to rooftops and cloudy skies. Finally, the cart stopped in a cobbled yard peppered with snow.

"This must be the town," decided the fir tree, remembering the sparrows and their stories. "But where are the decorations?"

The fir tree was unpacked from the cart, along with a dozen others, and they were lined up side by side against a brick wall, like soldiers on parade.

"What will become of me now?" wondered the fir tree, as a man looked them up and down. Every so often he stopped to admire one, holding it by its trunk and spinning it around. The man pushed and prodded at the branches of the trees, comparing how they matched from one side to the other.

When the man got to the fir tree, his face broke into a grin. He didn't need to spin this tree around or fuss over its branches.

"This looks magnificent! See how tall and even it is, and how green the needles are," he nodded. "Yes, I like this one. That's the tree for us!"

The man carried the fir tree across the courtyard, into a fine building with columns outside the door. Soon the tree found itself in a magnificent drawing room filled with oil paintings, sofas and a grand piano. A little crowd of children watched excitedly.

A butler in a smart jacket pointed to a beautiful bay window.

"Stand it up there," he said to the man. "Then we'll get started."

The children clapped their hands, cheered and skipped around with excitement. The fir tree was placed in a tub filled with sand, then a jolly green cloth was tied around the base.

"Now it feels like Christmas," smiled a young lady carrying a large wooden box. When she lifted the lid, the children gasped. Inside there were velvet ribbons and glass baubles, striped candy canes and fir cones painted silver and gold.

"Look at this," cried a young boy, picking up a tiny wooden reindeer. "May I put it on the tree?"

"Of course," replied the lady. "Gather round and join in, everyone!"

The Fir Tree

The boys and girls laughed and sang carols as they hung up sweets, garlands and pretty decorations. When they'd finished, the butler climbed a stepladder then gently placed a gold star at the very top. The fir tree was transformed. It had never looked so splendid.

"It's lovely!" smiled a little girl with rosy cheeks and a pretty white pinafore.

The tree listened as the butler knelt down to whisper in her ear.

"You wait until tonight," he said with a smile. "Tonight, this tree will shine from top to bottom!"

As the little girl's eyes filled with wonder, the fir tree felt another wave of anticipation ripple through its branches. It could hardly wait for the night to arrive!

"I wish the lights were lit already," it sighed, yearning to dazzle the room with its brilliance. The fir imagined itself shining brightly, adorned with beautiful trinkets and decorations.

"How long shall I be on display like this?" it pondered happily. "All winter perhaps? Maybe all summer, too?"

Soon it was time for the fir tree's big moment. It seemed to take an age for the butler and his servants to light up the decorations. The fir tree became brighter and brighter. Then people rushed into the room, holding hands and cheering at the sight. Reflections on the tree's glass baubles sent flecks of golden light spinning across the ceiling.

"It's the most beautiful thing I have ever seen!" declared the little girl with the rosy cheeks.

The children joined hands and skipped around the fir tree, pointing at the beautiful decorations. The stories, games and singing lasted for hours. Just before bedtime, the master of the house clapped his hands. The little ones rushed up to him, their faces pink with excitement.

"You've been very patient," he smiled. "Now it's time to take a trinket from the tree. Merry Christmas, everyone!"

A cheer rose up in the drawing room. The children jostled around the fir tree, standing on their tiptoes to pull presents and sweets off its branches.

"I hope they don't take many more," thought the fir tree. "My branches will soon be bare of treats!"

By the time the children had been carried up to bed, there was barely a present or sweet left on the tree. Instead of looking stately and fine, the fir tree felt dried out and thin.

"Never mind," it said, trying to comfort itself. "You can do it all again tomorrow!"

The fir tree dreamed all night about the fun it was going to have at the next party. The next night was sure to be its most glorious yet!

"Tomorrow I will look even more magnificent," it decided. "I shall play my part to perfection!"

In the morning, the fir tree watched a maid open the shutters in the drawing room. Stark morning sunlight streamed in through the windows.

"At last!" exclaimed the fir tree, standing as straight as it could. "Here I am, miss!"

The fir tree waited for the maid to stop and admire its handsome shape and colourful decorations. It waited for the children to come in and wonder with delight. It waited for more presents and sweets to be placed on its boughs.

And it waited.

Nothing happened. Without an upwards glance, the maid opened up a box filled with old newspaper. The surprised tree winced as she slowly and methodically pulled the remaining ornaments off it. Without further ado, each one was dusted off and packed away in the box.

The butler was called for. He took down the tree and dragged it out of the room.

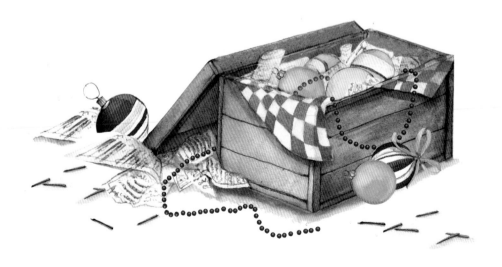

"What is the meaning of this?" the fir tree asked itself as it was bumped from stair to stair. A trail of brittle needles was left scattered on the carpet behind it. The butler shoved the tree into the attic, then locked the door.

It was lonely inside the attic. The fir tree was tucked behind a stack of boxes, hidden out of sight. It began to wonder if it had been forgotten.

After a while, the fir tree noticed a tiny crack in the rafters. If it leaned with all its might, it could just catch a glimpse of the world outside.

"It is still winter," said the fir tree, noticing the layer of frost that carpeted the garden below. "The ground is hard at this time of year. They must be waiting until the spring comes before they plant me again. Yes, that must be it! How thoughtful..."

The fir tree clung to this hope as day after day passed. In those quiet moments, it thought back to its time in the forest. The tree remembered the hare and the robin redbreast, and wondered if it would ever see the bird again or hear its merry song.

When the fir tree was at its most lonely, a tiny sound broke the silence of the attic.

"Hello, hello!" squeaked a mouse.

Another mouse and another appeared. Soon there were at least half a dozen. The little creatures darted up and down the fir tree, nestling in its branches and tickling its trunk.

"Where do you come from, old fir tree?" asked the mice.

The fir tree bristled. "I come from the most beautiful place – and I am hardly old," it retorted. "I've not even reached my prime! In the

forest where I grew up, there were trees much older than I am and not nearly as fine."

A white mouse twitched its whiskers inquisitively.

"Tell us about this beautiful place. Is it more wonderful than the food store full of shelves laden with cheese?" it asked the fir tree.

The fir tree told the mice about the hillside where it had grown up. It explained grandly how there were trees as far as the eye could see.

"How lucky you have been!" gasped the white mouse.

"That isn't all," agreed the fir tree, remembering the way that it had shimmered on Christmas Eve. "Did you know that I have stood in the best room of this very house, with a light shining on every branch?"

The mice squeaked in awe.

"It is true!" exclaimed the white mouse, scampering all the way up to the top of the fir tree. "Look – it's still got its golden star!"

The fir tree gasped. The mouse was right! The star was broken and wonky, but it was still just about in place.

Every day the mice brought more of their friends up to visit the fir tree. The little creatures curled themselves up tightly in its branches, tucked in side by side. They listened patiently to every detail of the fir tree's magical evening in the drawing room. It delighted in recounting the tale over and over, again and again.

"That was such a merry time," it would say wistfully at the end. "The happiest night of my life."

"Oh yes," said the mice, nodding their little heads.

The visitors all agreed that the fir tree had been very lucky indeed. After a while however, even the curious mice had heard enough. They

began to disappear back into the nooks and crannies from where they had come. By the time spring arrived, the fir tree was alone once again.

One fine morning, the attic door rattled open. The maid stuck her head in.

"At last!" cried the fir tree. "Now I can get back outside and start growing again!"

The fir tree felt itself being carried down the stairs, through the back door and out into the courtyard where it had stood months before. Outside the sun glittered and the cool air danced through its branches. The fir tree wondered where it was going to be planted.

But a different fate awaited the fir tree. The maid tossed it into a heap of nettles in the corner of the yard.

"This can't be right!" gasped the fir tree. "I still have lots of growing to do!"

The maid was gone already, rushing away to finish her chores.

As the fir tree lay on its side, it noticed how shrivelled it had become. Its lovely evergreen hue had faded into a dull brown. Its needles were almost all gone.

Noisy children clattered up and down the yard in their boots.

"Look at that old thing," they pointed, before snatching the battered star off its tip and running away.

Now the fir tree was filled with regret. How it missed the friendly little mice that used to tickle its branches! How it yearned for the peace and safety of the attic! Even those days were more wonderful than this.

"If only I had enjoyed my time on the hillside instead of wasting it," sighed the fir tree. "Every moment should have been a treasure."

With that, the gardener appeared. He used his axe to chop the tree up into pieces. The fir tree was thrown into the kitchen stove and burned.

There was no fanfare or ceremony. Yet as the wood crackled and popped in the grate, the fir tree saw things clearly for the first time. The tree gave thanks for the beauty it had seen in its life. It remembered the playful hare, the singing robin and the scent of the forest.

The fire faded to nothing. Out in the courtyard the children played on. The youngest boy laughed as he ran and skipped, clutching the star to his chest. Soon it would be another tree's turn to be admired. It would be crowned with the Christmas star, then stand glorious and majestic for one, perfect night.

The Snow Queen

Once there was a truly terrible hobgoblin. He crafted a mirror for himself that had strange and magical powers. Those who were beautiful appeared ugly and misshapen in its gaze – every flaw and imperfection magnified to a horrible degree.

In a faraway corner of the hobgoblin's realm, there was a school for imps. The hobgoblin held up the looking glass and gathered them around him.

"Look at this!" he crowed. "Nothing can escape its glare!"

The imps watched as the hobgoblin pointed his mirror down towards the Earth. The faces of the men and women below instantly became scornful and mean. The enchantment was so strong that their thoughts were changed too.

"Why should we be kind and good all the time?" they suddenly began to argue. "Nobody else is! We won't waste another minute thinking of anyone but ourselves. We don't like anyone else anyway!"

The mischievous imps flitted around the mirror, carrying it between them. Higher and higher they went, up into the sky.

"Who else can we point it at?" they shrieked, shining the glass back down towards the ground. "Let's do it again!"

The imps wrenched and tugged. The hobgoblin's mirror was pulled this way and that until it fell out of their grasp.

The looking glass smashed into a million tiny pieces, each no bigger than a grain of sand. The glittering shards were scattered far and wide. The specks flew through the air, spreading out into every corner of the world.

Instead of being disappointed, the hobgoblin was pleased – his mirror had become even more powerful than before. The shards of glass were so tiny they got into people's eyes, making everything they saw look bad and unpleasant. Some splinters even found their way into people's hearts. From that moment on they became cold and hard, unable to love anyone at all.

Far away in the big city, two houses stood side by side. A little boy called Kay lived in one house. A little girl called Gerda lived in the other. Kay and Gerda had been best friends ever since they could remember. Their houses were built so close together that they could see into each other's windows. In the mornings Kay would scramble over to the glass and wave hello to Gerda. She would always be there waiting for him, smiling her familiar, happy smile. At bedtime it was the same – Kay and Gerda never went to sleep without wishing each other goodnight.

In the winter when it was cold and ice frosted up the windowpanes, Kay would go and visit Gerda. The friends liked to sit next to each other in front of the fire, listening to Gerda's grandma. These were the times that Kay loved the most, as Gerda's grandma told the most magical stories.

"Look," she said one day, pointing to the snowflakes swirling outside. "The white bees are swarming!"

Kay and Gerda pulled their blankets over their knees.

"Do the white bees have a queen?" wondered Kay.

Grandma nodded. "Why, of course. The Snow Queen is always there, at the heart of every storm. On cold nights, she rushes through our city streets. Every time she stops to peer in a window, a silvery pattern appears. Can you see?"

Kay and Gerda rushed over to the window. The panes glittered as if they were covered with icy flowers. The children shivered when they thought of the Snow Queen passing by so close to where they slept at night.

Kay and Gerda's families shared a roof garden. When the summer came, the friends met outside on the terrace. Flowers trailed over the window boxes and green vines crept and curled across the tiles. Every year a stunning arch stretched from one house to the other, covered with scarlet roses. Kay and Gerda loved to sit under here, feeling the sun on their faces as they breathed in the scent of the flowers above.

One day, the friends were reading fairy tales together when Kay suddenly leapt out of his chair.

"Ouch!" he yelped. "There's something in my eye!"

Gerda rushed over to look, but when she checked, there was nothing to be found. Kay cried out again. This time he had felt an icy tingle in his chest.

"What's wrong?" asked Gerda.

Kay huffed grumpily, then elbowed Gerda out of the way so hard it made the little girl gasp in surprise. Something inside the boy had changed. A splinter from the hobgoblin's magic mirror had flown into his eye, and another had pierced his heart. Now when Kay looked up at the flower arch, he saw only maggots and dried-out leaves.

"What a horrible smell," he sneered, snapping a rose off and throwing it to the ground.

"Kay!" cried Gerda. "What are you doing?"

Kay crushed the rose with his foot, then ran inside. After that, he didn't want to play with Gerda any more. She still smiled and waved at him from her window every single day, but Kay never waved back. He thought her games were silly and he had no time for her grandma's stories. Every single day his heart grew colder.

By the time the winter frosts had started to return, poor Gerda was lonely and sad. Kay was always in a terrible temper, no matter what she did or said. One morning, she spotted him walking down the street, dragging his sledge behind him.

"Where are you going?" she asked. "Can I come, too?"

Kay didn't even stop to look over his shoulder.

"Leave me alone!" he snapped. "I'm off to the main square. I don't need a baby like you trailing behind me."

Kay stomped away. When he reached the square, it was covered with snow. Some big boys ran up behind the farmers' carts as they zigzagged across the cobblestones. If they were daring and quick, they could tie their sledges to the back of the carts and enjoy a ride around the streets.

Just then, a magnificent sleigh glided past. At the front, a silvery-white stallion snorted and tossed its head. Kay hitched his sledge onto the back of it and climbed on.

Swoosh!

The sleigh swept around the square so fast it took Kay's breath away. He held on tight as it turned off down a backstreet. The white stallion trotted on and on, faster and faster, until it finally broke into a canter and then a gallop. Kay tried to unfasten his sledge, but it was too dangerous. Before he knew it, he was being pulled out past the city gates and into the forest beyond!

"No more!" shouted the boy. "Please!"

The sleigh glided to a silent stop. A thousand snowflakes clustered together to form the shape of a tall, elegant woman. Kay saw the icy blue robes that she wore and her jagged, diamond crown. She could only be one person – the Snow Queen that Gerda's grandma had told him about.

The Snow Queen smiled at Kay, then bent down and kissed him on the forehead. Her kiss was colder than ice. The boy's heart was frozen solid. From that moment on, he forgot about Gerda, his family and his home. The Snow Queen helped Kay climb into her sleigh. Soon it had disappeared into the distance.

Gerda waited for Kay, but he did not come back. She walked round and round the square, asking everybody she met if they had seen her friend. She kept thinking of terrible things that might have happened to him, but her heart refused to believe it.

Gerda kept on walking and searching, until she found herself outside of the city, down by the river. The water was grey and cold, but there was a little rowing boat tied up amongst the reeds that lined its banks.

"I've run out of places to look," whispered Gerda, pushing the reeds aside. "Perhaps this river will carry me to Kay."

Gerda's heart thumped as she climbed into the little wooden boat. She summoned up all of her courage and pushed away from the bank. As the boat meandered down the river, she called out for Kay. She floated like that for many hours, until a pretty thatched cottage came into view. An old woman with a kindly face opened the door and beckoned as Gerda climbed out of the boat. She offered to feed the girl and give her somewhere to stay. The thought of sitting inside for a while was so tempting, but Gerda knew she had to get back in the boat. How could she stay when Kay was still out in the cold somewhere, all on his own?

After a while, a crow came to land by the side of the riverbank. As it hopped towards her, Gerda was amazed to discover that she could understand its squawks and cries.

"Where are you going, little girl?" asked the crow.

Gerda told the crow all about Kay, the boy she loved like a brother. The crow listened carefully to every word. At the end, it asked Gerda to come with him to a fine palace that stood close by.

"The palace belongs to a princess," the bird explained. "She got married only a little while ago to a young man who sounds just like your friend. My own wife-to-be lives there. She will find a way to let us into the palace, I am sure."

"Please take me there!" begged Gerda.

There wasn't a moment to lose. The crow hopped and fluttered over the snow with Gerda following behind. By the time they arrived at the palace, it was dark. Gerda crept in through a door where the crow's sweetheart was waiting to meet the little girl.

"This way," said the female crow, leading them up a twisty stone staircase. "Their Majesties have retired to bed."

Gerda picked up a lamp then made her way to a tall chamber at the very top of a high tower. A golden key hung on a nail beside the door. As quietly as she could, the little girl took the key and turned it in the lock, hoping against hope that Kay would be sleeping inside.

Two sleigh beds stood in the middle of the palace chamber beneath a crystal chandelier. A beautiful princess lay asleep on the bed nearest to the window, curled up under a rich plum eiderdown. Gerda shone her lamp onto the sleeping figure in the bed closest to her.

"Kay," she whispered. "Is that you?"

The figure turned over and stirred. In the half-light, his soft brown hair and peachy cheeks looked just like Kay's, but it wasn't him. The boy blinked in the lamplight.

"Hello," he smiled sleepily. "Who are you?"

The disappointment was too much to bear and poor Gerda burst into tears. The surprised prince sat up in bed, then called over to his princess. Together they rushed around the little girl, lighting candles, fetching handkerchiefs and begging her to tell them what was wrong. Gerda recounted her sad story from start to finish.

"Your poor thing!" declared the princess, brushing a tear from her own eye.

The prince and the princess pledged to help in Gerda's quest to find Kay. By the time the first morning light came streaming into the window, she was dressed in snug new boots and a warm fur cape. The royals led the little girl down to the palace gates where a brand new sleigh was waiting for her. It had been carved out of gold and harnessed to a fine grey mare. The horse's bridle was studded with glittering rubies.

Inside the sleigh, the servants had laid out sweets and gingerbread for Gerda to nibble on, as well as extra blankets to keep her warm.

Gerda climbed onto the sleigh and waved goodbye to her new friends.

"Thank you, Your Majesties," she called. "Thank you, everyone!"

"Farewell!" cawed the crows, gazing after the sleigh until it was just a golden dot in the distance.

Gerda's sleigh was sleek and fast. The mare galloped with ease, taking the little girl into the heart of a dark pine forest. The sleigh's gilded runners shone against the snow, lighting up the trails and pathways. Poor Gerda didn't notice the eyes peering out through the trees, watching greedily as she swept past.

"Whoa, there!" came a sudden cry.

A band of robbers burst out of the darkness, making Gerda's horse rise up in panic! Before she knew what was happening, the robbers had seized the mare and pulled Gerda out of the sleigh.

"This gold will be worth a pretty penny," snarled a robber, as he helped himself to the gingerbread and sweets.

Another pointed at Gerda.

"Take her back to our castle," he barked. "She'll make a useful serving maid."

Poor Gerda stood on the path, trembling with fear. Suddenly a girl about her age pushed her way to the front of the robbers. She was the daughter of the robber chief. The girl's hair was thick and tangled like a wild animal's, but there was a friendly sparkle in her coal-black eyes.

"Leave her alone!" shouted the robber girl to the gang. "She can be my playmate."

With that, the robber girl pulled Gerda back into the golden sleigh. They travelled together along a bumpy track. Wolves howled in the distance and ravens cawed as the sleigh wound its way up towards the robbers' castle – a desolate place guarded by fierce bulldogs.

As soon as they reached the castle courtyard, the robbers set about lighting a fire.

"This way," whispered the robber girl, leading Gerda inside a little outhouse, away from the rest of the robber band.

"Don't you get lonely here by yourself?" asked Gerda, staring up at the chilly rafters and bare stone walls.

The robber girl laughed then made a sudden cooing noise. A flock of pigeons fluttered in through the windows. They fluttered and strutted right up to Gerda, then pecked seeds out of the robber girl's hands.

"They are my friends," said the robber girl, proudly. "Bae, you can come out now too."

The robber girl picked up a coil of rope from the floor and gave it a gentle tug. An old shaggy reindeer appeared, dipping his antlers to nuzzle the robber girl's side.

"My animals sleep with me every night," said the robber girl.

Gerda was given some broth to eat and a blanket to cover her shoulders by her new friend. After a while, she didn't feel quite so scared. As the two girls sat side by side in the darkness, she told the robber girl all about her lost friend Kay.

Afterwards, the pigeons swooped down from their perches.

"We have seen this boy," cooed a dark bird with flecked feathers. "He was taken away by the Snow Queen."

Gerda scrambled to her feet.

"Where did they go?" she asked.

"She was on her way to Lapland," replied the pigeon. "Isn't that right, Bae?"

The reindeer nodded his head. He had been to Lapland many times. It was where the Snow Queen kept her summer palace.

The robber girl's eyes glittered with excitement. Quick as a flash, she untied the reindeer and pressed his reins into Gerda's hands.

"Goodbye, Bae," she said solemnly. "Take Gerda to Lapland. If Kay is there, you will find him."

Gerda was overwhelmed by the robber girl's kindness. Her new friend smuggled her out of the castle, past the dogs and the circle of thieves sleeping in the courtyard. She climbed onto the reindeer's back and galloped away.

"Can you see?" shouted Bae, as they thundered on, leaping over rocks and snow piles. "The Northern Lights are shining up ahead. That's the way to Lapland."

Gerda leant in and clutched the reindeer's fur. The sky glowed in shades of turquoise and violet, bathing the land in an eerie light. It was a long, cold journey, but the little girl never complained. Every minute was taking her closer to Kay.

Gerda and the reindeer ran on and on, until they reached a cottage with a lamp glowing inside. A wise old woman lived there. She opened her door and invited the travellers to rest for a while inside.

"Kay does not mourn for Gerda," she explained quietly to the reindeer. "There is a splinter of glass in his heart and another in his eye. While they rest inside him, he will never want to leave the Snow Queen's palace."

"Can you help Gerda to break this spell?" asked the reindeer.

The woman shook her head. "Gerda doesn't need any help – her love for Kay is strong enough," she said.

When Gerda was ready to leave the old woman's house, Bae took her to the edge of a vast frozen garden. On the peak of a snowy hill in the distance, she saw a shimmering palace sculpted out of solid ice.

"This is the Snow Queen's kingdom," said the reindeer, setting her down. "I can take you no further."

Gerda ran towards the palace on the hill. It stood tall and magnificent like a glacier, but its halls were cold and forbidding. As she stepped inside, Gerda didn't feel a shiver of fear. All she could think about was the joy of seeing Kay's face again.

In the very centre of the ice palace there was a frozen lake. The Snow Queen sat there on her throne, dressed in a flowing gown that shimmered with a million ice crystals. Kay knelt at her feet, still under her magical spell.

"Come along," called the Snow Queen, pointing to the floor. "Try and solve the puzzle."

Kay said nothing. He gathered up some jagged pieces of ice and started rearranging them, this way and that, on the floor. The shards were all part of a cruel challenge set by the Snow Queen.

"Just spell out the word ETERNITY," said the Snow Queen. "If you can do that, I will set you free."

Suddenly the Snow Queen swept out of the hall. Spring was coming. It was time for her to go and breathe cold winter air on the other side of the world. Kay was left alone with the ice puzzle.

At that moment, little Gerda found her way down to the frozen lake. "Kay!"

Gerda ran to her friend and put her arms around him. As she hugged him to her, teardrops rolled down her cheeks. The warm tears landed on Kay's chest, melting the ice in his heart.

"My friend!" gasped the little boy, as if he had come back after a long time away. He burst into tears, sobbing so freely that the ice was washed from his eye. The children laughed and cried with delight. Their joy made the Snow Queen's puzzle pieces leap and dance in the air around them. When they settled again, they spelled out the word ETERNITY. Kay was free.

Kay and Gerda walked hand in hand, out of the Snow Queen's icy realm. When they got to the edge of the palace grounds, the reindeer was waiting to take them back through Lapland, towards the city they had not seen for such a long time. He carried them for many miles, until the first new buds of spring appeared and the snow began to melt.

"Thank you!" called Kay and Gerda, smiling and waving. "Goodbye, Bae!"

With each new step the sun shone a little brighter, the grass grew a little greener and flowers began shyly to lift up their heads.

Rabbits scampered in the grass and new lambs played in the fields. It seemed that everybody was pleased to see Kay and Gerda back together again. Even the robber girl rode out on the grey mare to greet them.

"Well done, my friends," she cried happily. "One day, I'll come and visit you!"

Kay and Gerda walked on and on. They chattered all the way, remembering the happy times they had shared. Church bells rang and birds serenaded them as they went by. Many days passed.

One morning, Kay pointed out towards the distance.

"Look!" he cried eagerly. "There's our city. I can see the spires and the steeples."

Gerda laughed and nodded. The friends broke into a run, their hearts racing.

"There's the school, there's the market and – Kay," whispered Gerda, "there's the rose arch that grows over our roof garden!"

Gerda and Kay rushed over the hill, past the main square and through the narrow cobbled streets. The friends burst through Gerda's front door and leapt up the stairs two at a time.

"It's as if we've never been away," said Kay.

"Grandma!" called Gerda. "We're back at last!"

"Out here!" replied a happy voice.

Gerda and Kay stepped out onto the roof garden. There was Grandma, sat on her favourite chair underneath the rose arch! Her face lit up when she saw the children running out to greet her. She clasped their hands, then stared at them each in turn.

"I knew that you would come back to me one day," she said. "Let's sit out here for a little while. I've missed sharing stories!"

Gerda and Kay curled up at Grandma's feet. Sunshine danced on the roof tiles and the roses filled the air with their sweet perfume. Grandma sat back in her chair. She began to weave a wonderful new tale. As the friends listened, they forgot about the Snow Queen's cold and lonely heart. The memory melted away like a bad dream.

Gerda's eyes sparkled. Kay smiled. Their hearts were pure and true, just like they had always been.

"It's good to be back home," whispered Gerda.

Kay looked around him. He was warm, safe and content. Summer had come at last.

The Nightingale

Ancient China was a great empire – a land filled with glittering cities, snow-capped mountains and blue, snaking rivers. A long line of powerful emperors reigned over this vast kingdom, each more noble than the last. This story is about the very greatest of them all.

The emperor of China was a proud and stately ruler. His first decree had been to build a magnificent palace. Master craftsmen were brought from all over the kingdom – architects, carpenters, sculptors and artists. The palace was made from the most exquisite oriental porcelain. Delicately decorated walls glimmered as the emperor swept down the corridors in his fine silks, attended by an army of servants. A thousand priceless treasures adorned the sitting rooms and balconies. Every window overlooked the beautiful palace gardens.

"What a view," the emperor would say with joy. "It is without equal!"

The gardens were indeed a masterpiece. Their graceful walkways stretched as far as the eye could see in every direction. The paths were dotted with bridges and willow trees. The flowers were exquisite; frothy orange blossom, pale lilies and sweet-scented camellias grew in abundance. Gardeners tended the blooms, decorating their stems with tiny silver bells. As the emperor passed, the bells would sway in the breeze, making a charming tinkling sound.

The emperor's gardens were vast. Far, far away, at the very furthest reaches, stood a mighty forest. The trees were broad and tall, their branches entwined into a canopy of emerald green. The forest ran all the way down to the deep blue sea. There, by the water, lived a tiny nightingale.

The nightingale loved to sing. Every evening it would sit on its branch and warble in the twilight. As it sang, the bird's little chest puffed out and its eyes shone with joy.

Sometimes a poor fisherman would reel in his nets just below the nightingale's tree. The beautiful song would make him stop working and sit for a moment on the shore.

"I am alone," he would say, "and I have very little. Yet this dear bird makes my heart fill with happiness. What a rare gift it has!"

Talk of the emperor's spectacular palace spread far and wide. More and more sailing ships arrived, bringing visitors from distant countries. As the processions made their way through the forest, a lucky few would hear the nightingale's song.

The emperor's visitors admired the splendid porcelain palace and its stunning gardens. They walked along the blossom-lined avenues and listened to the tinkling silver bells. They stood on the dainty wooden bridges and gazed at the

lilies lifting their faces up to the sun. Every detail was heavenly and yet those that had heard it could not forget the sound of the tiny bird in the forest. After such beauty, nothing else could compare.

"The emperor has created a wonder," they would tell their friends, "but that nightingale in the forest! It is the very best of all."

The palace did indeed become a wonder of the world. Its beauty was held in such esteem, many wrote about it in their letters, poems and stories. The emperor liked to entertain himself by reading these books. How he loved to hear about his exquisite jade sculptures, fine tapestries and divine gardens. He would sit in his throne room, nodding his approval at each new line of praise. One day, however, a shout thundered out from the royal hall.

"What is this?" bellowed the emperor.

The lord-in-waiting rushed into the throne room. The emperor was holding a piece of parchment up with an angry, shaking hand. The parchment told of the matchless beauty of the nightingale's song.

"Why have I not heard of this creature?" said the emperor. "Strangers know my realm better than I do. I am humiliated!"

"Your Highness," grovelled the lord-in-waiting, making a deep bow. "Nothing is more beautiful than your palace. This book cannot be true. No one in court has ever seen such a bird."

"I must see it and I shall hear it sing!" snapped the emperor. "Find the nightingale and bring it to me, or the court shall pay the price."

The lord-in-waiting scuttled off in a terrible panic, shouting for butlers and footmen, gardeners and chambermaids. The servants ran

up and down the corridors searching hopelessly for the nightingale.

Every corner and every cupboard of the palace was searched. The day was drawing on, but the bird was nowhere to be found. The lord-in-waiting wrung his hands. The emperor could not be disappointed!

"This nightingale," he panicked. "It must be a silly fairy tale!"

A young kitchen girl happened to walk by, carrying a stack of dishes.

"I know the nightingale," she said, turning towards the window.

The lord-in-waiting was so relieved he could have jumped for joy!

"Speak!" he ordered. "If what you say is true, you shall be rewarded."

The kitchen maid put down her dishes. She gazed out across the palace gardens, towards the forest in the distance.

"My mother lives a long way from here," she began. "Every evening I walk through the forest to get to her little house by the shore. When I am at my most weary, the nightingale sings a song to cheer me. The music lifts my heart – I cannot describe the magic that it weaves!"

The lord-in-waiting clapped his hands. There wasn't a moment to lose! He called for a lantern, straightened his hat and rushed down the palace staircase.

"Come, little kitchen maid," he called over his shoulder. "We leave at once!"

The lord-in-waiting and the kitchen maid hurried through the palace gardens, followed by half of the court. They passed the formal lawns and the fountains, the tinkling flowers and pagodas, and eventually the path meandered into fields.

A deep moan rang out across the meadow.

"Is that the nightingale I hear?" cried a courtier. "How lovely!"

The kitchen maid shook her head.

"That's just a cow lowing in the field," she replied. "There is still further to go."

The group hurried on. The ground got boggier. The courtiers had to scoop up their robes to keep them out of the mud.

A rasping croak broke the silence.

Another courtier called out: "That must be it! How beautiful it is!"

"That is just a frog calling across the marsh," said the kitchen maid. "You will know when the nightingale sings."

The kitchen maid was right. When the courtiers reached the forest, the most marvellous music came to their ears. The nightingale's song was even more wonderful than they had imagined!

"Where is this creature?" asked the lord-in-waiting earnestly. "The emperor must hear its song."

The kitchen maid pointed up to a tiny bird perched in the branches above. The lord-in-waiting was expecting to see a spectacular bird, but this little creature was drab and brown. It was no bigger than the palm of his hand.

"Is it really you making that enchanting sound?" asked the lord-in-waiting.

"It is me," said the nightingale, fluttering closer. It bobbed its head, then sang again. Another melody danced through the forest, so clear and pure it made the courtiers gasp in astonishment.

"Little nightingale," the lord-in-waiting said solemnly, "please accompany us back to the palace. You must entertain the royal court with your charming song."

"I am just a bird," the nightingale replied quietly. "My music sounds best amongst the trees of the forest."

The lord-in-waiting pressed his hands together, then bowed his head low.

"My master has asked to hear your song," he said. "It is his express wish."

When it heard that, the little bird was overwhelmed. How could it refuse the emperor of China?

"It would be an honour," it chirped. "I shall come gladly."

And so the tiny, drab little bird was taken to the palace. As the nightingale fluttered into the court, a throng of elegantly dressed courtiers and ladies bowed before it. The room was full to bursting – even the kitchen maid had been allowed to come into the throne room and hear the visitor's song.

"What a splendid place!" thought the bird, taking in the sight of gleaming porcelain walls, rich tapestries and a thousand golden lamps flickering from the ceiling. Exotic flowers decorated with tinkling bells had been brought in from the palace garden, filling the chamber with a heavenly scent. The nightingale felt a long way from its shady home in the forest.

The lord-in-waiting clapped his hands. The room instantly fell silent.

"Dear nightingale," he said politely. "May I present you to His Imperial Majesty, the Emperor of China."

The courtier pointed to a small golden perch positioned in front of an ornate throne. A little man sat there, impatiently tapping his fingers.

"I am pleased to meet Your Highness," said the nightingale, taking its place. Without further ado, it held up its head, puffed out its chest and sang.

The room was spellbound. The little bird sang so gloriously, it was as if the world had stopped for a moment. When the nightingale looked at its host, the emperor was overcome. Tears of joy streamed down his cheeks.

The nightingale sang again. This time the melody held such tenderness it touched the emperor's very heart.

"Enchanting!" he exclaimed, leaping up from his throne. "The most enchanting sound I have ever heard."

The nightingale bowed its head modestly, and when the emperor offered rewards of coins, gifts and trinkets, it refused.

"I have seen tears of joy spring to the emperor's eyes," it warbled gently. "What further reward could a little bird need?"

The visit was a success, but when it was time for the nightingale to leave, the emperor jumped to his feet. He summoned the lord-in-waiting to his side.

"The nightingale cannot leave me," he announced. "It shall live here in the palace. Make it so."

The lord-in-waiting bowed his head. The emperor could not be denied.

And so the nightingale didn't go back to the forest. Instead it lived in a gilded cage. The lord-in-waiting saw that the little bird had the best of everything. A dozen servants attended to it, offering sweetmeats and titbits whenever it desired. The nightingale had a beautifully detailed perch, crafted from solid gold.

Twice a day the cage door was opened, but the bird never strayed far. It had no choice – the servants each held onto a fine silk ribbon tied around its leg.

The bird never complained, but its eyes grew sad. It missed the dappled light of the forest and the hush-hush sound of the ocean waves breaking on the shore.

One day the lord-in-waiting brought in a parcel for the emperor. It was a gift from the Emperor of Japan. Inside was a mechanical bird made out of silver and gold. It was the same size as the nightingale in the cage, but this bird wasn't dull and brown. Its gleaming body and wings twinkled with precious gemstones.

The emperor was filled with joy by his new toy.

"I wonder if it can sing?" he mused. "Call the music master."

The music master was an elderly man with a very long beard. He examined the mechanical bird closely, then wound up a cog at the front. The model nightingale began to sing a pretty little tune, bobbing its tail on every beat.

The people in the court clapped politely and nodded their heads.

"Now let's hear it sing with the real nightingale," said the emperor.

The emperor's servants opened the door of the nightingale's cage. The music master tapped his baton, then pressed a button at the back of the model bird. The mechanical nightingale and the real nightingale began to sing, both beautifully, but not together. The model nightingale performed the same song over and over again, but the real bird sang from its heart, changing the tune as it pleased.

"We cannot blame the mechanical bird," insisted the music master. "It was a textbook performance!"

The music master wound the cog up again and set the artificial bird singing on its own. The bird sang at least thirty times, without pausing or tiring. The emperor and his courtiers listened spellbound, marvelling at the rubies and sapphires glittering all over its body. Nobody noticed the real nightingale hop off its perch and fly away, back to the forest.

When the emperor did at last look up and spot the empty cage, he frowned in disappointment.

"Why would the nightingale want to leave me?" he asked. "After everything that I have done for it, too."

The lord-in-waiting and the music master fussed around the emperor. They convinced him that the model bird was far superior to the dowdy little creature that had entertained him before.

"The jewelled nightingale will never let you down," insisted the lord-in-waiting. "It is perfect and predictable."

The music master nodded his head. "The model bird is a mechanical masterpiece. It is a gift fit for an emperor."

And so the emperor did not mourn the loss of the little nightingale. Instead he demanded a public concert to show off his new toy. Everybody in the palace poured into the throne room to listen to the dazzling mechanical bird. The chamber rang out with the sound of applause.

The concert was a dazzling success. People clamoured to praise the newcomer's glittering decorations and intricate song. Only one person did not make a fuss about the mechanical bird – the poor fisherman who had heard the real nightingale singing down by the shore. He'd come to the palace to sell his catch and been drawn into the performance. The fisherman listened. This bobbing and whirring machine looked very fancy, but it didn't quite have the magic of the true nightingale. Something was lacking.

After that, the emperor banned the real nightingale from ever returning to the palace. "A dull brown bird doesn't belong in my fine chamber," he scoffed.

The lord-in-waiting placed the mechanical nightingale on a velvet cushion beside the emperor's bed so that he could gaze at it every day. It became the emperor's most prized possession. He invited overseas visitors to the palace just so they could witness its splendour. The artificial bird was even given its own royal title – 'Grand Imperial Lullaby Singer to the Emperor of China'.

News of the mechanical bird spread. After a year, many books and journals had been written about it, which pleased the emperor enormously.

One night, however, the unthinkable happened. The bird was entertaining the emperor with its usual song when something inside the machine snapped. *Ting!* The cogs inside the nightingale juddered to a stop. The artificial bird's lovely music was replaced with an empty click-clicking sound.

The emperor's eyes filled with dread. He couldn't do without his nightingale! He called for his lord-in-waiting. The lord-in-waiting called for the music master. The music master called for the watchmaker.

The watchmaker took the mechanical creature apart, cog by cog, spring by spring. His fingers trembled with anxiety as the emperor leaned over his shoulder, watching every move. Slowly, carefully, he repaired the break and put the tiny parts back in again.

The emperor smiled when the mechanical bird started to sing again. "It is fixed!" he declared, clapping his hands.

The watchmaker coughed nervously.

"The bird is fixed for now," he warned, "but the parts inside are worn out and cannot be replaced. If Your Majesty winds up the cogs too often, they will break completely and the nightingale's song will be lost. The bird can only be played once a year, if at all."

The emperor was very disappointed. From now on he would have to do without his bedtime lullabies – he could only gaze at the jewelled nightingale instead.

Five years passed. It was not a happy time for the emperor. Every day he grew weaker and paler. Eventually he became so ill he was confined to his bedchamber. The great ruler of China was now a wizened figure lying in the middle of an opulent four-poster bed, looking upon the mechanical nightingale.

The palace courtiers grew more and more worried about the emperor's health. A throng of people gathered outside the palace gates, waving flags to wish him well and cheer his heart.

Soon the emperor had grown so cold and lifeless he could barely breathe. The lord-in-waiting began to plan for his master's succession. A new emperor was lined up to take his crown. Courtiers and servants waited in silence. Outside in the palace gardens, the silver bells were cut from every flower so that His Majesty would not be disturbed.

One evening, a full moon cast its silvery light into the royal bedchamber. The emperor was so close to death, he could barely lift his head up to look out of the window. His feverish mind was overcome by dark and terrible nightmares. When the emperor could stand it no longer, he stared across at his jewel-encrusted nightingale and begged it to sing.

The bird, of course, stayed silent. It was fragile now and there was no one there to wind it up. The emperor closed his eyes in despair and sank his head into the pillow.

"This must be the end," he sighed. "No one can hear me and there is nothing left to live for."

But someone had heard the emperor. Suddenly a blissful harmony floated in on the evening breeze. There was the real nightingale, perched on a blossom spray outside the palace window!

"You came back," whispered the emperor, his eyes filling with tears.

The nightingale sang on. Its melody had never sounded more tender or more beautiful. The emperor's nightmares faded into the shadows and he felt comfort in his heart. The colour began to return to his face. The fever had disappeared.

"I do not deserve to hear your sweet music," said the emperor humbly. "How can I repay you for this kindness? Let me give you a home in the palace. I will surround you with all the gold and jewels you could ever wish for."

"I do not wish for gold or jewels," replied the nightingale. "And I cannot live in a palace. Knowing that I have touched your heart is all the repayment I need."

The emperor's face paled again. He knew he could not do without the nightingale's lovely song. The bird fluttered closer.

"I will still visit you," it said gently. "Let me come and go to the forest as I please and every evening I will perch on this tree and sing about what I have seen. I will tell you about the people that I meet – the merchants, the farmers and the lowly fishermen on the shore. Your porcelain palace is very fine, but you are surrounded by courtiers that simply want to please you. I will sing the truth – happy and sad – so that you can rule this kingdom fairly and with all your heart."

The emperor's face filled with happiness. He promised to keep the nightingale's visits a secret, before sinking into the sweetest, most peaceful sleep he had ever had.

The next day, the lord-in-waiting crept nervously into the emperor's bedchamber, wondering whether his master had made it through the night. He blinked in surprise. His Imperial Majesty was up, dressed and standing in front of the window!

"Good morning, dear man!" the emperor cried, his face filled with smiles. "Let's get to work. I have a kingdom to run."

The Princess and the Pea

nce upon a time, in a land of rolling hills and bubbling streams, there was a castle. The castle was many hundreds of years old, and its ancient ramparts bore the scars of countless battles lost and won. It had a great stone keep, an oak drawbridge and a moat that swirled all around it. Every turret and spire of the castle was decorated with fluttering gold flags. When the sun shone and a fair breeze blew, the flags waved and sparkled for all to see.

A king and queen lived in the castle with their only son, the prince. They were good and fair rulers, and the kingdom was prosperous. Every day, crowds of villagers would cross the moat and ride into the castle grounds to sell their wares. The courtyards rang out with the sound of laughter as friends greeted one another and swapped news.

The king and queen were growing old. It wouldn't be long before their son, the prince, would need to take up the throne. But before he became king, the prince wanted to find a princess to be his wife.

"Our son is handsome, brave and clever," said the queen. "Yet he is still unmarried. The years rush past, but there is no sound of wedding bells."

"We must send our son out into the world to seek his bride," announced the king. "The royal courts are full of princesses and one of them will surely be perfect."

"What an excellent idea," agreed the queen. "Summon the prince!"

The prince agreed at once to his parents' proposal. Letters were immediately sent to all the finest royal kingdoms, announcing the prince's intention to visit.

"I shall voyage to every corner of the globe," he promised. "I will know my princess when I see her!"

The prince wasted no time in preparing for his journey. The finest stallion in the land was groomed and saddled, then brought out to the castle courtyard. The drawbridge was lowered.

The king and queen watched from the tallest turret as their son galloped away from the castle. They did not know when they would see him again.

The prince was gone for many months. He travelled to the snowy peaks of the north. He explored the mysterious Orient and its palaces. He visited desert kingdoms and feasted in the greatest citadels of Arabia. He was welcomed at many fine courts. When the prince explained his quest, his hosts hurried to present their daughters to him. Many of these were gifted and fair. Many had grand titles and wealth. Yet not one of these, in the prince's eyes, was the princess he yearned for.

When he could, the prince wrote letters home. As soon as the queen spotted a messenger riding through the valley towards the castle, she would scurry down the stairs in a fluster.

"This must be it," she would exclaim. "The news we have been praying for!"

The king would follow slowly behind, hoping the queen was right. Each time, the royal pair sat side by side on their thrones and waited for the messenger to open his scroll.

"His Majesty is in India," the messenger said one day. "The sultan has shown him great hospitality. When the prince arrived, a carnival was held in his honour. There were streamers, dancers and parading elephants."

The queen waved her handkerchief in delight.

"How wonderful," she gasped. "And what about the sultan's daughter? I have read all about her. She is said to be the jewel of India!"

"She is indeed very fair, Your Highness," replied the messenger. With that, he coughed nervously and stared down at the floor.

"Well?" demanded the king. "When is my son bringing his bride home?"

The queen leaned forward in her chair.

"The prince has refused to ask for the princess's hand," said the messenger in a quiet voice. "He says that what she boasts in beauty, she lacks in grace. He could never marry such a person. She is not a real princess."

The messenger rolled the scroll back up again and retreated from the throne room.

As the days and weeks passed, every letter the prince sent home was the same. Despite this, he kept searching.

The prince travelled to Bavaria. A duke invited him to a glittering ball, attended by a thousand noble guests. As the violins played, the prince stood on the palace balcony with the duke's daughter. She was both witty and fair, but she talked endlessly. Her chatter skipped and dipped like butterflies flitting in the wind. The prince did not ask her to marry him. In his heart he knew that this young lady was not the real princess he searched for.

The Fairy Tales of Hans Christian Andersen

The prince rode on, towards the gleaming domes and spires of Russia. The empress was thrilled when she heard of his visit and an audience was arranged without delay. She was fabulously wealthy and had many fine palaces. Dozens of suitors had already offered their hand to her in marriage. Yet the prince did not make a proposal. The empress's riches had made her haughty. She screeched at her servants and would only eat food presented on a solid gold platter. This was not the real princess that the prince had been dreaming of.

The prince rode away with a heavy heart. There was nowhere else left to go. He turned his horse back towards home.

Every morning, the queen sat in her turret, gazing towards the horizon. She longed for news of her son. One morning it was the prince himself who rode towards the castle, rather than a messenger.

"He's home!" she cried, tugging at the king's sleeve. "There he is!"

The prince's stallion walked slowly up through the valley. He looked up at the king and queen, then waved forlornly.

"The prince is alone," sighed the king. "He's not met his princess."

"I searched everywhere but couldn't find a real princess," said the prince, "and I cannot marry anyone else. I am sorry."

"Don't worry," said the king, welcoming him inside. "She'll come along one day."

"We will just have to be patient," nodded the queen.

And so the king and queen continued their reign. The kingdom was peaceful. There were harvests and holidays, markets and feasts – just as there always had been. The prince gave up on his quest for a princess

and devoted himself to the people. When the villagers came to the castle, he spent time talking to them and helping them with their problems.

One day, dark clouds stole over the valley. Thunder rumbled in the distance. Rain lashed down. The villagers fled home to their cottages. They brought in their animals and closed their shutters and doors. A storm was on its way.

The hours ticked by. A chill breeze whistled round the castle. By nightfall it had spun itself into a terrible gale. The prince paced the castle's stone passageways, helping servants bolt gates and tie down trapdoors.

"It is a fearsome night," the prince remarked, stopping to peer out of a window. A jagged lightning bolt splintered the sky.

The king and queen stoked the fire in the little room that they were sheltering in.

"Hurry son," called the queen. "Come and sit with us in the warm."

The king pulled a rug over the queen's knees. "I pity any poor soul out in this storm tonight," he added.

But as the prince took his seat, something extraordinary happened. Three faint knocks could just be heard above the noise of the storm.

Knock, knock, knock.

"Did you hear that?" asked the queen.

"Hear what?" puzzled the king, who was a little hard of hearing in his old age.

"I heard it. But no one would be knocking on the door on a night like this," replied the prince. "It must be the thunder."

Bang! Bang! Bang!

This time there was no doubt. Somebody was at the castle door!

The king rose to his feet. "We must let them in and offer them shelter," he decided, "whoever they may be."

The prince helped his father pull open the castle's great oak doors. To their astonishment, a girl was standing outside.

"Good evening," she said politely. "May I please come in?"

The prince could not take his eyes off the stranger. She looked so beautiful standing there, even though she shivered in the cold night air. The girl's simple gown was drenched in rainwater and her thin shawl clung to her shoulders. Her tresses hung in damp curls around her waist. Even her dainty slippers were splattered with mud.

"Dear child," said the king. "What are you doing out in this terrible storm?"

"I was travelling when I lost my way," replied the girl. "Then I saw your castle and hoped you might allow me to shelter for the night. I am a real princess, you see. As soon as daybreak comes I'll be on my way again."

The king spluttered in surprise. A real princess? He rushed upstairs to tell the queen as fast as his old legs would carry him.

"Forgive my father's manners," said the prince, reaching for the princess's hand. "Please let me show you inside."

While the queen rushed off to make preparations for the princess, the prince invited the visitor to sit beside the fire.

"Thank you for your kindness," said the princess, curtseying gracefully before sitting down.

The prince felt his cheeks flush. Something about this visitor made his heart tingle. He hadn't noticed until now what beautiful green eyes she had. The princess's auburn hair tumbled in waves around her shoulders, shining in the glow of the firelight. He felt as if he could never tire of the princess's company. She had all the qualities of a real princess – she was kind, clever, funny and thoughtful.

Meanwhile, the queen lit a fire in the guest bedroom and fetched soft blankets and towels. Next she filled a bath full of bubbles and precious flower oils. Then she ran down to the kitchen to find something hearty for the princess to eat.

"Poor thing!" she muttered, bustling up and down the castle steps with armfuls of eiderdowns and extra flagons of water for the bath. "Look how she shivers with cold! We must warm her up."

"Her clothes are simple and plain," whispered the king. "And yet she claims to be a princess. Can that really be true?"

The queen smiled knowingly.

"Leave this to me," she replied. "I was a princess once and I know the perfect test. By morning we shall know the truth about our mysterious stranger."

"Your bedchamber is ready for you," said the queen at last. "Come this way."

The princess followed the queen up a narrow, winding staircase. At the very top was a candlelit room with soft fleeces spread across the floor. The princess smiled gratefully when she saw the sweet-scented bath that the queen had filled for her. Clean night robes had been put on a table, along with a delicious bowl of hot chocolate. The rest of the chamber was filled with an immense four-poster bed. The princess gasped. There had to be at least twenty mattresses piled onto the bed, stacked up in a dizzying tower!

"I do hope that you will be comfortable," said the queen, pointing to the giant bed. "We don't often have princesses to stay at the castle."

The princess rubbed her eyes.

"I'm certain I will, Your Majesty," she said. "I am exhausted!"

The queen chuckled quietly to herself as she closed the princess's door. The visitor couldn't know what else the queen had prepared for her. At the very bottom of the bed, the queen had placed a single, tiny green pea.

"Sleep well, fair stranger," she mused. "Let's see if you are a real princess."

The king, queen and prince were eating their breakfast when the princess appeared the next morning. The storm had blown over and sunshine streamed in through every window. Outside, the castle's gold pennants fluttered in the breeze.

"Good morning," said the prince, leaping to his feet at the arrival of their guest. "Please join us."

The princess stifled a yawn. She looked just as lovely as she had the night before, but her face seemed pale. There were dark shadows under her eyes.

"How did you sleep?" asked the king.

The princess looked at her lap.

"Please tell us," said the queen, gently taking the girl's hand. "Don't be shy – you can speak openly with us."

"I don't want to appear ungrateful," said the princess quietly. "You've welcomed me in so graciously."

"Not at all," comforted the queen.

"There was a hard lump in my bed," the princess finally admitted. "I'm bruised black and blue from it. You've been so kind, but I couldn't sleep a wink."

The prince frowned with concern. But the queen had heard everything that she had hoped for. Much to the princess's surprise, she hugged her tightly.

"We have found our real princess!" she beamed. "Only a *real* princess would be delicate enough to feel a tiny pea through so many mattresses. Your precious bride has come to you at last, son!"

"I knew it!" laughed the king.

The prince dropped down onto one knee. He had loved the princess from the moment he'd opened the castle door and seen her standing there, shivering in the rain.

"Would you do me the honour of marrying me?" he asked.

The princess's eyes sparkled with happiness.

"Yes," she nodded. "I will!"

The king and queen could rejoice at last. There was going to be a royal wedding!

The prince married his bride that very day. Every man, woman and child in the kingdom joined in the celebrations. Throughout the valley church bells rang out. The newlyweds stood arm in arm on the castle ramparts, waving to the people below. The king and queen could rest at last, for the prince and his real princess were destined to live happily ever after.

This tale is true, but it happened a long time ago. If you are passing by the castle, be sure to visit its museum. There is a very special exhibit on display. It's right at the back, in a dusty glass case. Peep inside and you'll see the proof of a *real* princess – a tiny, shrivelled pea.

The Steadfast Tin Soldier

Once there was a little boy who lived in a grand townhouse at the end of a leafy avenue. The house had a painted gable along its rooftop, gleaming windows and a very smart entrance hall. Fine carpets lined the staircases and chandeliers hung from the ceilings. It was a very happy home.

On the boy's birthday there were treats, balloons and a magnificent cake covered in candles. His family sang 'Happy Birthday' to him in the morning and his friends came round for a party in the afternoon. Afterwards, the boy was led up to the playroom on the top floor. He gasped when he saw the colourfully wrapped parcels piled up on a chair. The boy undid ribbons and opened packages, his eyes glittering with excitement. Finally he got to the present from his parents.

"Tin soldiers!" cried the boy, tearing the wrapping paper off a large wooden box. Inside was a regiment of men-at-arms. All twenty-five soldiers were painted in a smart livery of blue and red. They wore tall plumed hats and carried muskets by their sides.

"Look how they stand to attention," marvelled the boy, setting them up along the playroom floor. "Thank you Mama, thank you Papa!"

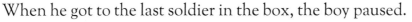

When he got to the last soldier in the box, the boy paused.

"Oh!" he said. "This soldier has only one leg."

The soldiers had been cast from some old tin spoons. There hadn't been quite enough metal to finish the last man and so the toymaker had tucked him away underneath the rest. Despite missing a leg, the tin soldier stood upright and steady.

"This one must go on parade, too," decided the boy, placing the soldier in line. "He is just as smart and brave as the others."

The boy spent the rest of his birthday evening playing with his new toys. The soldiers waged wars against teddy bears, then knocked down building bricks with their muskets.

At the other end of the playroom there was a fine wooden castle in silver and white. It had little windows, hand-painted bricks and blue flags posted on every turret. Around the edge of the castle was green felt grass. When the tin soldier with one leg was carried past the toy castle, something caught his eye.

"Oh my!" he gasped to himself.

There, standing in the doorway, was a beautiful ballerina dressed in a delicate pink net tutu. Her arms were outstretched and for a moment the soldier imagined that she was reaching out to him. She wore a sash over her shoulder, fixed in place with a glittering star. The doll had only been fashioned out of paper, but the soldier thought she was the prettiest thing he'd ever seen. The ballerina had one foot pointed out behind her in a graceful arabesque.

"She stands on one leg, just as I do," marvelled the soldier. "What a wonderful wife she would make!"

But then the soldier scolded himself. How could a lowly tin soldier dare to dream about such a dazzling ballerina? Such a refined lady would be much too grand for him!

"She lives in a silvery castle, while I am packed tightly in a box," sighed the soldier. "Twenty-four other soldiers elbow and nudge me all night long. That is no place for an elegant lady. It cannot be!"

The evening drew on and it was soon time for the boy to go to bed. Before the boy packed up his birthday presents, the tin soldier tucked himself behind a box on the windowsill.

177

"I'll hide away here," said the tin soldier, gazing over at the ballerina.

The boy placed the rest of the soldiers back into their box and closed the lid, forgetting the twenty-fifth man with the missing leg. He ran out of the playroom, closing the door behind him.

Suddenly there was a muffled cry from the toy chest in the corner. The lid was thrown open and a colourful nutcracker doll appeared.

"Bedtime at last," he shouted. "Toys – come out to play!"

The playroom erupted with a clatter of shouting, crashing and banging. It was pandemonium! The train set whirred and clicked, music boxes played and bouncy balls jumped off their shelves. The rocking horse pranced around the room with the nutcracker riding on

his back. Ragdolls held tea parties and wooden animals scattered in all directions. The twenty-four tin soldiers heard the noise from inside their box. They wanted to play too, but it wasn't to be – no matter how hard they thumped and rattled, the lid was shut tight.

The games got rowdier and rowdier. The nutcracker stampeded across the playroom, raising a battle cry as he waved his fist. It was a wonder the family wasn't disturbed!

In the face of all this commotion, the one-legged tin soldier stood silent and still. In her castle, the ballerina was frozen too, fixed in her pose. The soldier and the dancer stared into each other's eyes all night long, not turning away for a moment.

Dong! Dong! DONG!

The grandfather clock in the hallway struck midnight. All of a sudden the box by the soldier flipped open. A jack-in-the-box sprang out, bouncing back and forth, its mouth stretched into a wild grin. It had scarlet cheeks and a bright jester's hat made from clashing pieces of velvet.

"What have we here?" cried the jack-in-the-box. Its spring squeaked noisily as it bobbed about in front of the tin soldier. "Turn away from the ballerina! She doesn't want to have a broken soldier staring at her all night long."

The tin soldier refused to take his eyes off the paper ballerina. Her arms reached out to him just as before.

"What do you say, little soldier?" prodded the jack-in-the-box. "Answer me!"

The tin soldier stayed steadfast. He did not utter a word. The jester sneered and coiled back into his box, vowing to make the tin soldier pay for ignoring him.

When morning arrived, the toys became motionless once more. A maid came into the playroom. She cleaned out the fire grate, then opened the windows to let in the morning air.

As soon as the maid's back was turned, the jack-in-the-box burst out of his box. He knocked into the tin soldier with such force that the one-legged figure was sent flying out of the window. The soldier turned head over heels time and again, tumbling down to the street below.

"Goodness gracious!" cried the maid, peering over the windowsill.

The jack-in-the-box cackled with glee as the flustered girl rushed out of the playroom. She ran down the stairs, meeting the little boy on the way. Together they went into the street to search for the missing toy.

The poor soldier had landed with a terrible bump. His hat was tightly wedged in a gap between the paving slabs and he couldn't wiggle free. All that could be seen was his one leg stuck upright in the air.

The boy and the maid scoured the pavements outside the house. They walked straight past the stranded soldier several times, but he was too small for them to spot lodged in amongst the stones. The soldier refused to cry out for help, for the boy and maid couldn't know that he talked. Besides, that was not what a soldier would do.

"I am a man in uniform," he told himself firmly. "We do not make a lot of fuss and bother when times are hard."

After a while, it started to rain and the maid led the boy back inside. The soldier felt each raindrop running down his leg and dripping off his musket. The downpour got heavier and heavier. The crack in the paving stone began to fill with dank grey water, raising the soldier up a little.

"What's that?" came a voice once the rain had stopped.

A boy crouched down on his haunches just above the crack in the pavement. He beckoned to another boy in a grubby woollen sweater. Together they used a stick to give the toy soldier a prod.

"He's only got one leg!" exclaimed the first boy. "Let's get him out!"

The two lads poked the soldier out of his hiding place, then brushed the dirt off him with the backs of their hands. Then they began to play.

When they'd tired of marching the soldier up and down the pavement, they made a boat out of an old sheet of newspaper.

"Time to go!" shouted the boys, dropping the soldier into the paper boat. Before the soldier could work out port from starboard, the boat was set upon the water streaming in the gutters and sent sailing towards the drain.

"Stand tall," whispered the tin soldier, staring out across the prow of the boat. He tried his best to stay upright as the boat whirled round and round in the current. The rush of water felt like a tidal wave! The soldier nearly fell overboard countless times, but he clung on tightly to his musket and refused to move. As the water eddied and churned beneath him, he remembered the dainty ballerina. How he missed her already!

Whoosh!

Suddenly the rainwater river tipped into an inky black hole and the paper boat was washed into a drain below the street. The soldier held on helplessly, knowing that he was moving even further away from the lovely paper dancer.

"Who goes there?" demanded a voice in the gloom. "This is my drain. You need to pay to pass this way!"

An oily-looking sewer rat swiped at the tin soldier with its claws, just as the paper boat lurched out of its reach. The boat swept ever onwards, away from the rat and on towards the town sewer.

After a little while the soldier spotted a chink of light, far off in the distance. The water gushed faster and faster and swept the paper boat towards the light. The tin soldier felt dizzy as he watched twigs and pieces of litter being dragged over the edge of a drop into a wider channel beneath. The noise of rushing water grew into a deafening roar.

"This is it," said the soldier, as the paper boat teetered on the edge of the drop. "I am surely done for. Straighten up soldier, and meet your fate with courage!"

There was no hope of escape. The boat lurched forwards, then dropped. It turned over and over through the spray, down and down towards the whirlpool below. The tin soldier held his musket up and pushed out his chest. He was certain that he would never see the ballerina again, but her sweet image gave him the strength he needed to stand tall.

The boat plunged into the swirling canal and the tin soldier felt icy water rush over his head. The paper boat became wet, turned to pulp, then broke apart. The soldier was left sinking, helpless and alone.

A huge silvery shape swam by the sinking soldier, its scales glinting in the half-light. A beady eye darted left and right.

Gulp!

The fish swallowed the soldier whole, flared its gills, then plunged back down into the depths from where it came.

It was blacker than the toy box inside the fish's belly. The soldier was cramped and frightened, but still he stood to attention. Somehow he managed to straighten his little hat and mount his musket back up on his shoulder.

"I am a soldier," he told himself. "It is my duty to be brave."

The fish twisted and turned in the water. Every move bent and squashed the soldier. But just when he was certain that he would be crushed, the creature became still. The soldier waited and waited. He did not cry out and he did not close his eyes.

A knife cut into the side of the fish above the soldier's head, chased by a flood of light.

"Good heavens!" a voice cried. "Our lost soldier!"

The tin soldier blinked, then looked around him. Instead of a sewer, he found himself stretched out on a block next to a bubbling stove. A plump cook with ruddy cheeks gawped down at him.

A maid peered over the cook's shoulder. The tin soldier recognized her as the same girl that had opened the window in the playroom.

"What lucky chance is this?" gasped the tin soldier. "I have come back to where I started!"

The toy was quickly washed, then taken back to the playroom. The boy of the house was overjoyed to see the soldier again.

"You must go where I can always see you," decided the boy, putting him down next to the toy castle.

The tin soldier held his head up high. His heart nearly burst when he looked across and saw the paper ballerina standing there too, just as she had always done! Her tiny star glittered and her net tutu rustled around her. She had never looked more enchanting. The soldier and ballerina stared longingly into each other's eyes.

Lots of the boy's friends came to visit the plucky tin soldier. They gasped when the boy told them how the toy had been discovered in the belly of a fish!

But one of the boy's friends didn't like all the attention the tin soldier was getting. Recklessly, the visitor picked up the toy and threw it into the fire.

"No!"

The boy reached out to save his toy, but it was too late. The tin soldier was already melting in the flames. The ballerina watched helplessly from the table, desperately fixed in her graceful pose.

The steadfast tin soldier stood to attention one last time. His eyes held no anger – they were full only of love and admiration for the little paper dancer.

Suddenly a breath of wind curled in through the window, lifting the ballerina off her feet. She twirled up through the air like a feather, before gliding down into the flames beside the soldier. The paper flared up for an instant, then disappeared. At the same time, the tin soldier melted into the coals.

The next morning, the maid came to clean the grate as usual. There, amongst the ash, were two tiny treasures.

"A heart made of tin and a sparkling star," she exclaimed, plucking them out of the cinders. "How pretty they are! I'll keep them safe."

The maid blew the coal dust off the heart and the star, then placed them both in her locket. A little part of the tin soldier and his paper ballerina were together at last.

The Storyteller's Story

Hans Christian Andersen (1805–1875) was born over 200 years ago, but the magic in his fairy tales sparkles down through the generations. The stories are vivid and rich – bustling with strutting emperors, shimmering mermaids and tiny people no bigger than your thumb. Hans's imagination was so inspired, it could even give a voice to a lonely fir tree or a little tin soldier with one leg.

Sometimes Hans compared his own life to a fairy tale. It certainly began in poverty, as the only son of a shoemaker and a washerwoman. His childhood in Odense, Denmark, was difficult and lonely, but he always knew that great things lay ahead of him.

Hans wrote poems, acted and sang whenever he could, determined to find fame and fortune. When he was thirty years old, Hans wrote a collection of four fairy tales. This little book secured his future as a master storyteller. No one had seen anything like it before – Hans's tales read as if he were sharing a favourite bedtime story. Each story featured enchantment and wonder, but also a delicate balance of light and shade. Many of his tales don't have a traditional happy ending.

The storyteller had a way of filling his adventures with deeper truths about life, perhaps writing a little of himself into each tale. Hans has often been compared to the gawky mistreated creature in *The Ugly Duckling*. At first he was certainly an outcast, but just like his famous hatchling Hans was destined to blossom in a way that would astonish everyone.

Hans wrote over 160 stories. During his travels around Europe, countless children and grown-ups fell in love with his work. Soon royal heads of state were seeking out his company, listening enraptured as he read his books out loud. By the time Hans died in 1875, Denmark had honoured him as a national treasure.